LETHAL IN SMALL DOSES is the fourth book in a murder mystery series by best-selling author David Pearson. Details about the first, second and third books, A DEADLY DIVIDEND, A FATAL LIAISON and THE CHINA CHAPTER, can be found at the end of this one.

A list of characters has also been supplied at the back of this book.

Part One

Chapter One

Detective Sergeant Fiona Moore sat at her desk in Store Street Garda station. It was ten in the morning, and it seemed to Moore that she was being totally overpowered by paperwork. She hated it. Her inbox had no less than fourteen emails from the administrative side of An Garda Síochána, covering everything from health and safety to overtime use for the last month in the unit, and a plea from management to try and curtail it.

It was high summer, and as a result the workload for the detectives in and around the city was less than at other times of the year. It seemed that many of the criminal classes were away on expensive foreign holidays, and while the city was thronged with tourists, most of the petty crimes involving them were dealt with by uniformed officers.

Moore hadn't had her summer holiday yet. She was booked to travel to Majorca with her sister later in the year when school children had returned to study, and the price of airline seats and hotels had eased back to a manageable level for a Detective Sergeant's budget. She had taken a few days on her own over in the west of Ireland just after Easter to indulge her photography hobby, but it seemed a long time ago now as she opened yet another email from Garda HQ and studied it.

Her boss, Detective Inspector Aidan Burke, suffering fewer financial constraints, was indeed on his holidays. He had gone initially to England where he hooked up with his brother, Cormac, and his family. They had set off to France by train where Cormac had a modest cottage close to Carnac in Brittany with its stunning sandy beach. Since his divorce, Burke had been at somewhat of a loose end when it came to holidays, so Cormac tried to include him whenever possible, and it worked well, as Aidan was popular with Cormac's two children, Aoife and Shane.

Moore's phone rang.

"Good morning, Fiona. It's Malcolm here from the mortuary. Have you got a minute?"

The caller was Dr Malcolm O'Higgins, the State Pathologist, who worked very closely with the Gardaí when suspicious deaths, or worse, came along. He was a dry sort of character who used irony and humour to make his grim job a little more tolerable, and was a damn fine pathologist with a good instinct for malfeasance.

"Hi, Doctor, sure, what's on your mind?"

"I have the body of a woman here who was brought in last night from a nursing home out in Glenageary. She was apparently in rude health according to the staff at the facility, but was found dead in her bed close to midnight last night. She hadn't seen a doctor for some months – hence the need for a post-mortem."

"I see. So, what's the issue?"

"We've been doing all the normal things, and to be truthful, I wasn't expecting to find anything unusual. But when I was just about to slice her open, I noticed what may be slight bruising in the thorax area, and there is some sign of petechiae on the face and a little conjunctiva in the eyes."

"In English, please, Doc."

"Oh, yes, sorry, bloodshot eyes and broken small blood vessels in the face. Not very pronounced, but unusual all the same."

"Do you suspect foul play, Doctor?"

"I'm not sure, but it may be a possibility. I'd welcome your opinion."

"OK. Give me fifteen minutes and I'll come across."

"Fine. See you then, and if you happen to be passing a coffee shop on the way over, mine's a latte with two sugars," O'Higgins said.

"What does Claire take – in coffee I mean?" Moore said.

"Oh, she's an Americano type."

"I'll bear that in mind," Moore said, rolling her eyes to heaven.

But in truth, she was delighted to have an excuse to abandon her current task, and while she was not at all sure that O'Higgins had uncovered anything sinister, she would enjoy the break away from her desk.

* * *

O'Higgins had his pathology laboratory in a building behind the City Morgue on Amiens Street. It was just a short walk from Store Street Garda station where Moore worked, and conveniently, there were two excellent coffee shops en route.

She arrived at the pathologist's sterile workplace armed with three coffees and an equal number of doughnuts that she had purchased in Insomnia.

"Very kind of you," O'Higgins said, standing back from the gurney, where the hapless woman was laid out, to remove his gloves and wash his hands.

He took his cardboard cup of coffee, and handed the third drink to his assistant, Claire who was standing nearby.

"So, what have you got?" Moore said, removing the white plastic lid from her own drink and carefully sipping the piping hot liquid.

"Meet Mrs Fidelma Humphries, eighty-four years of age next birthday, and resident of the Cedar Hill home for the retired in Glenageary until yesterday."

The woman who was positioned on her back with a support under her head and a white muslin cloth covering much of her body, had a full head of blue-grey hair, which had clearly been well looked after. Her skin was wrinkled, but not excessively so for a person of that age, and although she was somewhat overweight for what Moore guessed would be her five-foot four inches height, she was by no means obese.

O'Higgins put down his drink and came back to the table.

"As I was saying, if you look very closely you can see what I was talking about on the phone," O'Higgins said, pointing with the tip of a ballpoint pen at the woman's face.

"Hmm... OK. Anything else?"

"Yes," O'Higgins said. "Look here. There are some marks beginning to appear around the neck area. It's not much, I didn't see it at first, but there's definitely something. It's not typical of a natural death from, say, heart attack or stroke."

"And what would this evidence lead you to believe happened to her, Doctor?" Moore said.

"That's for you to find out, Sergeant. I just cut them up and make observations," O'Higgins said, reaching for his drink again and standing back rather smugly.

"But give me a clue. Are we talking suffocation?"

"It's certainly a possibility. We have to do the tox analysis yet, and I'll know more when I get her opened up.

It could just possibly be a massive heart attack. That sometimes produces similar symptoms – but not the marks around the neck. That's different. I'll be writing it up later on, and I'll send across my full report, but I thought you might need to get on it a bit quickly, if indeed there has been foul play. And anyway, I was dying for a coffee – if you'll excuse the expression," O'Higgins said.

"Very droll, Doctor, very droll. Well, I'd better go and see what I can find out, hadn't I?" Moore said, collecting her things and heading for the door.

Back at the station, Moore collected Detective Dónal Lawler from the open plan office that they both worked in.

"C'mon, Dónal, we've got a house call to make out in leafy Glenageary. I'll drive."

Chapter Two

It was a fine bright morning as the two detectives drove out through Merrion Square and on via Ballsbridge to Blackrock, where Moore selected the Bray Road to take them up through Monkstown Farm and into Glenageary. Monkstown Farm was definitely not any kind of farm. It was now covered in vast numbers of what had once been council houses, but had been sold off mostly to their tenants some years ago. It got its name from a previous incarnation, when it had been farmland belonging to the Boley estate, the seat of Sir Valentine Grace, which covered hundreds of acres in the area during the nineteenth century.

There was no sign of any cedar trees, and definitely no hill, when Moore pulled up outside the Cedar Hill nursing home on Ormond Road. The home was comprised of what had been two separate, magnificent, semi-detached three-storey red brick houses with granite steps up to the front. Each property was double-fronted. The first property had a large bay window to the left of the front door, which was mirrored by a similar one in the second house, but on the right of the entrance. Both had woodwork that was painted in matching navy blue, and highly polished brass fittings adorned the entrances. There was an old cast iron boot scraper strategically positioned outside each, set into the granite doorstep.

"Looks expensive," Moore said getting out of the car.

As they walked across the immaculate pea gravel and climbed the steps, a discreet brass plate fixed to the wall indicated that one should enter the premises by the left-hand door.

Moore went ahead of her colleague, and was surprised to find that the front door was wide open, and that an inner glazed door was also unsecured. She turned the round brass knob and pushed it open. Inside, a wide, brightly tiled hallway led away to the back of the house, where a small mahogany reception desk with a lamp had been positioned. The smell in the place was that peculiar blend of old people, cleaning products, disinfectant and potpourri so common in these kinds of establishments.

The two detectives advanced down the hall to the reception desk which was unattended. Kitchen noises could be heard coming from downstairs, and in one of the rooms to the right of the hallway, the sound of a television set blaring out some inane game show was presumably keeping some of the inmates amused, or at least distracted from their situation.

Moore and Lawler stood at the desk for a few minutes, but still no one appeared.

"This is nuts. The place is wide open. Anyone could come in or out without being seen," Moore said. "You wait here – I'm going to find someone."

Just then, a young girl in a royal blue housecoat came down the stairs carrying a bundle of sheets.

"Excuse me," Moore said, "we're looking for the manager, or the owner. Could you get them for us please?"

"Who are you?" the girl said rather curtly in a distinctly Eastern European accent.

Moore took her warrant card out of her jacket pocket and held it up for the girl to see.

"Police. Now if you could just get someone to speak to us, please."

"OK. I'll get Mrs Phillips," the girl said rather nervously and disappeared downstairs into the basement of the building.

Moore and Lawler spent several more minutes waiting at the reception desk, looking around making their own observation, before Mrs Phillips arrived up from downstairs.

"Good morning," the woman said extending her hand towards Fiona Moore, "I'm Marjorie Phillips, how can I help?"

Introductions were completed, and then Moore said, "Is there somewhere private we could have a chat, Mrs Phillips?"

"Yes, yes of course. Come into the office."

The office was a room off the hallway at the back of the house. It was a square room with a dark red carpet, expensive curtains, and was filled with a large antique desk and a number of mahogany chairs in the style of old dining room furniture with leatherette seat cushions and ceramic casters.

The window in the room looked out over a very well-tended rear garden featuring a good-sized patio close to the house where three of the residents were taking morning coffee seated around a white wrought iron Victorian styled table.

Mrs Phillips sat in behind her desk which had a PC, a phone and several files piled up on one side.

The woman looked at Moore expectantly.

"Mrs Phillips, I understand you had a Mrs Humphries with you until last night, is that correct?"

"Oh, yes. Poor Fidelma, she passed yesterday. She was a lovely woman. Hadn't been here that long – let me see – just over a year, I think. She'll be missed – she was quite a character."

"Had she been in good health?" Lawler asked.

"Yes, she had. We were very surprised to find that she had died so suddenly. But it's not unusual in our business. I'm sure you understand."

"Had Mrs Humphries been on any regular medication, Mrs Phillips?"

"Oh, I'm not sure I can discuss that with you, Sergeant. You know – patient confidentiality and all that," Phillips said.

"Are you medically qualified, Mrs Phillips?"

"Well, no, I mean I have a first aid qualification, and of course I have been on courses on how to manage the elderly, but I'm not a doctor or anything."

"Then maybe you could just check Mrs Humphries' medication for us? I can assure you, there's no need to worry about confidentiality," Moore said, looking sternly at the woman.

Mrs Phillips woke her PC up by moving the mouse around on the desk, and typed something into the machine.

"Hmm... let me see, well she was taking statins – we recommend all our residents to check with their doctor about that, and she was on a very mild dose of blood pressure medication. That's it. Nothing major."

"Presumably these were prescribed by a doctor?" Moore said.

"Yes, of course. We allow our residents to use their own doctor if they want to, or if not, we have a doctor on call here all the time. We use Dr Fleming. He lives nearby and is very attentive."

"Did Mrs Humphries have her own doctor?" Moore said.

"No. Well, not recently, anyway. But she was very healthy. She didn't need one."

"Who renewed her prescriptions then?" Moore said.

"Dr Fleming. He does that for any of our residents that need it," Mrs Phillips said.

"Surely he needs to see them first?" Lawler said.

Mrs Phillips shuffled uneasily in her chair, and looked down, avoiding eye contact with the detective.

"Not always, no."

"Did Mrs Humphries have any relatives?" Moore said.

"Yes. She had two sons and a daughter. The sons visit regularly, but I think the daughter lives down the country somewhere, so she only makes it up once a month or thereabouts."

"Do you have any addresses for them?" Moore said.

"Yes, we keep a record of next of kin. Hold on, I'll print them off for you."

Mrs Phillips tapped a few more keys on her computer keyboard, and a page issued from a small black printer on her desk. She handed it to Moore.

"How many residents do you have, Mrs Phillips?" Lawler said.

"We're licensed for twelve, but our normal compliment is ten. We have four bedrooms in this house and six next door. We have converted the reception rooms in the adjoining house to bedrooms. The dining room and day room are both here on the ground floor."

"May I ask who administers the medication?" Moore said, anxious not to get side-tracked.

"We have two fully trained nurses on staff, Sergeant. Paula works from eight in the morning to four in the afternoon, and then Sally takes over from three-thirty to eleven-thirty. That gives a half hour hand-over and ensures that we always have a nurse on hand."

"What about weekends and through the night?" Lawler said.

"We use agency staff on Saturday and Sunday. None of our guests are terribly ill, Sergeant, so apart from the porter, we don't have any staff on during the night. It's never caused us a problem."

"And where are the medicines kept, Mrs Phillips?" Moore said.

"They are all locked away securely in a cabinet downstairs. I oversee the measuring out with the nurse before I go off in the evening, and we record it all in a logbook as well. It's all right and proper. I'm very fussy about that. But why all the questions? Surely Mrs Humphries died of natural causes?" the woman said.

"Just routine, Mrs Phillips. We always have to submit a report in these cases. I wonder if we could see your medicines cupboard?" Moore said.

"Well, yes, I suppose so, if it's absolutely necessary. It's downstairs."

Moore got up and gestured with her head to Lawler when Mrs Phillips wasn't looking. Then she accompanied the woman downstairs through a series of narrow corridors, into the kitchens, and on into a small storage area where fresh linens and a small array of medical supplies were stored.

"Here we are," Mrs Phillips said, pointing to a white metal cabinet fixed to the wall with a large green cross on its door.

"And where is the key kept?" Moore said.

Mrs Phillips reached up to the top of the cabinet and fetched a small key, holding it up for Moore to see.

"I have a spare in my office in case this one gets mislaid."

Moore took the key and opened the little cupboard. Inside were three rows of packets and bottles, all clearly labelled. On the bottom shelf there were a number of hypodermic syringes with needles, wrapped in a plastic bag and secured with an elastic band.

Moore took out her mobile phone, and much to the surprise of Mrs Phillips, took a photograph of the inside of the cabinet.

"I suppose everyone knows that the key is kept up there?" Moore said.

"Possibly. But only the nurses and myself are allowed to use it. Everyone knows that."

"I see. Before we go, could I ask you to give me details of all your staff, Mrs Phillips."

"Yes, I suppose so. But is there something you're not telling me, Sergeant?"

Moore ignored the question and the two women climbed back up the stairs to the reception desk where they encountered Lawler just finishing a conversation with a pretty, petite woman in a nurse's uniform.

"Thanks, Paula. See you again," Lawler said.

They waited another few minutes and Mrs Phillips re-appeared from her office and handed Moore two sheets of paper, stapled in the top corner.

"Thanks," Moore said, "we may need to come back to talk to the other nurse and the porter at some stage. We'll let you know. Oh, and could I ask you not to disturb Mrs Humphries' bedroom until you hear from us. I'd like it locked," Moore said.

"That's a bit awkward, Sergeant. You see, we have a waiting list for Cedar Hill, and there's another resident due to move in tomorrow. We'll have to get the room deep cleaned, and all the personal items removed before he gets here."

"Well, I'm sorry, but I'll have to ask you to put him off for a day or two. It can't be helped. Tell him there is some maintenance needed, or something. We need to get our forensic people out to go over the room."

Mrs Phillips looked very uneasy at this suggestion, but finally agreed saying, "Very well, if you insist. But I wish you'd tell me what's going on. It's most unsettling."

"All in good time, Mrs Phillips. Now we best be off. We'll be in touch soon."

Chapter Three

"What did you make of that?" Moore said when they were back in the car, driving towards Dublin.

"It's crazy. The place is more or less open to the four winds. Anyone could get in and out unseen. I was asking Paula about CCTV – I spotted a camera in the hall," Lawler said.

"What did she say?"

"It doesn't work, apparently. Never has. Not as long as she's been there anyway."

"Terrific! Any thoughts?" Moore said.

"We need to get to speak to the family, as well as the night nurse. She must have been on duty when they discovered Mrs Humphries," Lawler said.

"Agreed. You seem to have a way with the nurses. Why don't you come back out at around five o'clock and interview Sally, and while you're at it have a chat with Mrs Phillips about security. Offer to get the Crime Prevention Unit out to help her secure the place. It's daft the way it is. And while you're there, talk to the night porter too. Bring someone with you who can help you go over Humphries' room as well. Bag up anything that seems out of the ordinary, and take her pillows away. We need to get them examined."

"OK. What are you going to do?"

"I'm going to start some background work on the family. I don't want to move in on them yet. Not until Dr O'Higgins has confirmed that it wasn't natural causes, in any case. I wish Aidan Burke was here. This is all a bit above my pay grade."

"Ah, you'll be fine. Don't forget to put the Superintendent in the picture. You know what he's like."

"I suppose. Though we haven't really got anything to tell him yet. Oh, and see if you can get to talk to that Dr Fleming. He might be able to tell us something – and he seems pretty handy with his prescription pad. Rattle him a bit. Find out a bit more about who's getting what drugs, and why," Moore said.

"Good idea. I'll give you a call after I've spoken to them later on."

* * *

When Moore and Lawler got back to the station, there was a message for Moore that the Superintendent was looking for her. She put her jacket on the back of her chair, and went upstairs to Heffernan's office.

Superintendent Jerome Heffernan was originally from Cork. He had been obliged to come to Dublin to further his career when there were no suitable vacancies in the Southern Division of the Garda Detective Unit. He was a shrewd man, and had impressed Garda management with his ability to get results, and was considered to be a safe pair of hands with some of the more delicate cases that presented themselves in central Dublin. He had managed a nasty business involving espionage and drug smuggling from China very sensitively, where an airport worker had been killed, and as a result was generally left to his own devices by the Assistant Commissioner to whom he reported. But he knew only too well that each new case had its pitfalls, and if any of his charges were to slip up during an investigation, he would soon get it in the neck from on high.

Moore knocked on Heffernan's door.

"Come in, Fiona. Take a seat. How are you managing with Aidan away?" he said, signalling her to be seated in front of his generously proportioned and clutter-free desk.

"Fine thanks, sir. So far anyway."

"Look, I've had a call from Dún Laoghaire. Detective Inspector McNabb. He's not too happy. Apparently there has been a suspicious death at a care home in Glenageary, and he's wondering why the hell we have our size nines all over it. What's the story?"

Moore outlined how Dr O'Higgins had called her early that morning to share his suspicions about the death of Mrs Humphries, and she had just picked it up and ran with it. She didn't mean to cause difficulty.

"Well, be that as it may, McNabb's nose is a bit out of joint. What's the story on the woman's death, anyway?" Heffernan said.

"I'm just waiting for Dr O'Higgins's report, sir, but it looks like she may have been murdered all right."

"I see. Well you may be in luck, Sergeant. McNabb is short-handed too this week. I'll probably be able to keep him quiet. But not for long. Can you handle this if it is a murder?"

"Yes, I think so. I have Dónal Lawler with me," Moore said.

"Very well. Be sure to keep me informed, won't you. And if it goes into next week, we may have to let Dún Laoghaire in on it, and fight over who gets the spoils."

Heffernan then looked down at his desk and started reading some papers – the universal signal that the meeting was over.

"Yes, sir. Of course." She got up and left.

* * *

"Dr Fleming's surgery," the well-spoken girl said when Lawler rang the number.

"Hi. This is Detective Dónal Lawler from Store Street Garda station. I was wondering if it would be possible to see Dr Fleming this afternoon at all?"

"Just a moment, please."

Lawler could hear keys clicking on the girl's computer as she looked through the doctor's diary.

"I could fit you in at four-thirty for fifteen minutes if that's any good. What seems to be the problem?" she said.

"Oh, I'm not sick. I just need to talk to Dr Fleming about an enquiry I'm working on."

"Very well. Four-thirty then. See you later."

"Thanks. See you."

* * *

Moore sat down at her desk. She could do without the extra pressure of having Heffernan breathing down her neck and some inspector from Dún Laoghaire wanting to bump her off the case, but she was determined to make a go of it, if for no other reason than to impress DI Aidan Burke when he got back from his holiday.

She took the information about Mrs Humphries' next of kin that she had been given at the retirement home. She started with the two sons, Stuart and Dylan. Moore had always found LinkedIn to be a very good source of information, so she logged in, and it didn't take long to locate Stuart Humphries. Thankfully, there was only one person by that name listed for Dublin.

Stuart was in insurance. He had a full biography on his posting, which showed that he had previously worked for two of the largest general insurance companies in the country before setting up his own brokerage firm in Blackrock, called, not surprisingly, Humphries Insurance Brokers. Moore then went onto Google and brought up the company's website. She learned that Humphries not only dealt with the run of the mill products such as household and motor, office and shop insurance, but he also appeared to have a line on event insurance. Moore's curiosity was piqued, so she dug a little deeper. She found a description of the service spelled out in enticing language:

> *Organising a weather dependent event? Did you know you can insure against bad weather, poor attendance or even outright cancellation? We cover everything from Garden Fetes to International Sporting Fixtures. Competitive premiums offered. Give Stuart a call today to discuss your specific requirements.*

Moore was completely unaware of this type of insurance cover, and wondered what the premiums would run to, and who underwrote the risk.

Moore clicked back to the home page of the website and gave the office a call.

When she asked to speak to Mr Humphries, the girl on the phone said, "I'm afraid Mr Humphries isn't in the office today. He's out on family business. I can put you through to Derek if it's an insurance quote you need?"

"No, it's fine, thanks. I need to speak to Mr Humphries himself. I'm from the police. I wonder if you could give me a contact number?" Moore said.

"Hold on a sec," the girl said, and then reeled off a mobile number which Moore wrote on her jotter.

Moore called the number. It was answered immediately by a well-spoken man with a deep voice.

"Mr Humphries, this is Detective Sergeant Fiona Moore from Store Street Gardaí. I'm sorry to disturb you, and I'm very sorry for your loss. I wonder if it might be possible to meet you today – just for a few minutes?"

"Hello, Detective, yes, I'd like to meet you. In fact, I was about to call the Gardaí myself. What time suits?"

"I could do it now, Mr Humphries, if that suits. Where do you suggest?"

"I live in Killiney, and I guess you're in town – let's meet halfway. What about the Mespil Lodge Hotel on the canal? I can be there in twenty minutes."

"Fine. I'll see you there. Thanks."

Before Moore left the station, she got a message to call Dr O'Higgins.

"Yes, Doctor, what's up?" she said.

"Hello, Sergeant. Thanks for calling. I thought you might like to know that we found traces of morphine in Mrs Humphries. Not a large dose, but enough to render her unconscious for quite a while."

"Really! Wow. OK, thanks, I'd better get the full forensic team out to go over the room. It's clearly murder now."

Chapter Four

Dónal Lawler arrived back out in Glenageary at just before four-thirty. He found Dr Fleming's place easily. It was a modest 1960s semi-detached house on St Catherine's Road, and it looked as if Fleming had converted the garage into a surgery, and lived in the remainder of the house himself. A black two-year-old Audi A6 was parked in the driveway.

The surgery had a separate door with an illuminated plastic sign overhead – presumably to prevent endless callers to the house looking for the good doctor.

Lawler left his car outside on the road, and walked in. The surgery door opened directly into a very small reception-cum-waiting room area with a small desk and six plastic chairs positioned around the walls. There was a low table in the centre with the inevitable motley collection of dog-eared magazines, including several copies of National Geographic with their characteristic bright yellow cover.

The receptionist was seated at a very crowded desk that just managed to accommodate her PC, two telephones and two bright red stacks of filing trays which were themselves packed to the brim with manila folders.

Lawler introduced himself to the woman.

"Yes, officer. Dr Fleming is just with his last patient for the day. He'll see you in a few minutes. Take a seat," she said, indicating the vacant chairs nearby.

After a few minutes, a door off the reception area opened, and a woman in her seventies emerged, followed by a tall, lean man wearing a brown suit and glasses. The doctor saw his patient to the door, and turned to greet Dónal Lawler.

"Come in, Detective," he said extending his arm to usher Lawler into the inner sanctum.

The consulting room was small, but bright and relatively cheerful considering its purpose. There was a narrow trolley-bed along the wall behind the door, covered in absorbent white paper. It had a screen a bit like a shower curtain that could be pulled around to afford some basic privacy, and the curtain itself looked clean and fresh.

Dr Fleming's desk was largely clutter free, except for a PC and a phone, and to its left, there was a cabinet with glass doors housing an array of medicines that were neatly arranged. A wash hand basin on the other side of the desk, and a device for measuring blood pressure fixed to the wall completed the furniture in the small room.

When they were both seated, Fleming asked, "Now, how can I help you today, Detective?"

"Firstly, thank you for seeing me at short notice, Doctor. I understand you look after some of the residents of Cedar Hill, is that right?"

"Well, yes, sort of. A few of them have their own doctor, but I tend to the medical needs of a small number of them all right. They don't require much, in all honesty. Mrs Phillips only takes in fairly healthy people," the doctor said with a wry smile.

"Was Mrs Humphries a patient of yours?" Lawler said.

"Yes, if you could call it that. She was in remarkably good health until – well, you know."

"When had you last visited her?"

"I'd seen her when I was there last week calling on Mr Vincent – he's not so well I'm afraid. We exchanged a few words, but it wasn't a consultation. Fidelma was in the day room chatting away to some of the others, and I just said hello out of politeness."

"What medication was Mrs Humphries on, Doctor?"

"She took statins to keep her cholesterol down, and I had her on a mild dose of perindopril. She was inclined to be a little hypertensive – but nothing serious. If she had lost a few pounds of weight it would probably have resolved itself, but Fidelma liked her food."

"Did you ever prescribe morphine for her?"

"Good Lord, no. She had no need of it. Her joints could be a little bit stiff occasionally – normal for someone of her age – but nothing unusual, and she had no other condition that would demand morphine. Why do you ask?" Fleming said.

"Our pathologist, Dr O'Higgins, found traces of morphine in her blood."

"Well, she certainly didn't get it from me!"

"What's your opinion of the regime up at the home, Doctor?" Lawler said.

"How do you mean?"

"I was thinking about medication generally, and the administering of it. Anything out of the ordinary that you might have observed?"

"No. Nothing. They have some fairly potent stuff on-site. But Mrs Phillips has two very capable nurses working there, and the drugs are kept under lock and key. What are you implying?"

"Nothing. I'm just trying to get a picture of the operation. I may as well tell you, Doctor, we are treating Mrs Humphries' death as suspicious."

"I see. That's disturbing, Detective. Are you saying she may have been murdered?" Fleming said, looking quite shaken.

"That's what we need to find out. How long have you been attending Cedar Hill?"

"Let me see. It must be eight or nine years now – yes, nine years altogether. I started when Mrs Phillips took over. I think it might have been a guest house before that."

"And have there been many deaths at the place?"

Fleming looked at Lawler and smiled.

"That's the normal exit route for old people in a retirement home, Detective. So, yes – there have been several. But there's never been any suspicion of foul play up to now. Are you sure about this?"

"We'll know more as our investigation progresses, but it looks likely. But I'd like you to keep this conversation totally confidential for now, Doctor. We don't want to start a panic or even any speculation."

"Of course – mum is the word."

"Right, well thank you for your time, Doctor. I may need to speak to you again, and if anything occurs, please be in touch," Lawler said handing over one of his cards, and getting up to leave.

"OK. Let me know how things move on, won't you?" Fleming said.

Lawler just smiled and shook the man's hand.

* * *

By the time Dónal Lawler got to Cedar Hill, it was after five o'clock. He spotted the white 4x4 used by the Garda forensic team parked on the driveway. Once again, the doors to the place were open, and again there was no one in attendance at the reception desk. The residents seemed to be having their evening meal. Lawler could hear the clatter of cutlery and crockery coming from the dining room.

Lawler loitered in the hallway for a few minutes until a woman in a blue nurse's uniform came down the stairs. The nurse was in her late twenties or early thirties with long chestnut hair tied back in a ponytail. Lawler was immediately attracted to her.

"You must be Sally," he said extending his hand as she landed at the bottom of the stairs.

The woman held out her own hand rather hesitantly, and said, "Yes, but who are you?"

Lawler introduced himself and asked Sally if there was somewhere they could have a word in private.

"Yes, sure. We can use the office. Mrs Phillips has gone home. She's very upset about poor Mrs Humphries."

The two of them went into the office and sat opposite each other in the visitors' chairs in front of the desk.

"How can I help you?" Sally said.

"Mrs Phillips told us this morning that you would have administered Mrs Humphries' medication last night. Is that right?"

"Yes, that's right. She normally went up to bed at around 9:45 after the evening news on the TV and I would go into her room at around ten and give her her tablets and settle her down for the night."

"Tell me about last night, Sally. Was there anything unusual at all about it?"

"No, nothing. Everything was perfectly normal, until later, when I found her."

"How did that come about?" Lawler said.

"At about twenty past eleven, Mr Kendrick rang his bell. He has a room on the same landing as Mrs Humphries. I went to see what he wanted, and when I was leaving his room I heard the radio in Mrs Humphries room was on, and it seemed to be tuned to a pop station. That was very unusual – Mrs Humphries only ever listens to Radio 4. So, I knocked on her door, and when there was no reply, I went in, and there she was. I knew straight away that there was something badly wrong, so I checked for a pulse and then called the ambulance."

"What did you think had happened to her?"

"I didn't know. She was in pretty good health generally, but I know she was on blood pressure medication. Maybe a stroke, or a massive heart attack."

"Did you notice anything odd about the room at all?"

"What sort of thing?"

"Anything out of place, or not where it ought to have been?"

"No, it all seemed fine, except for the radio. As you can imagine, I was more concerned about Mrs Humphries than anything in the room. But I didn't notice anything out of place."

"Do many of the residents here pass away suddenly, Sally?"

"Well, yes, I suppose so. Not as suddenly as that, though. We usually transfer them to hospital, or the hospice if they get very ill. It doesn't do morale any good if there are deaths on the premises."

"OK, thanks. I need to go and talk to the forensic team – I presume they are upstairs in Mrs Humphries' room. From what you say, there may have been someone in there that shouldn't have been. And maybe you could let Mrs Phillips know what's going on for me?"

"Yes, yes, OK. But will that delay things a lot?"

"How do you mean?"

"It's just that we have a waiting list, and there's a new resident due to move in tomorrow to Mrs Humphries' room. We usually do a deep clean first of course, and then get the new patient to come in at around 4 p.m."

"We have asked Mrs Phillips to put that off for a day or two. By the way, did Mrs Humphries ever get any morphine?" Lawler said.

"No, not from me anyway. But I don't think she needed it in any case. Why do you ask?"

"Ah, probably nothing. Do other patients have it?"

"There is one resident that has it prescribed. He gets injections from time to time. I don't like it though, but his doctor insists," Sally said.

"Would that be Dr Fleming?"

"No. He has his own doctor. A Dr O'Malley. I don't like him much either, but don't say I said."

Lawler tapped the side of his nose.

Chapter Five

When Moore walked into the reception area of the Mespil Lodge, Stuart Humphries was already standing there looking out for her.

They introduced themselves, and sat down in the lobby of the hotel, which was very quiet at that time of day.

Stuart Humphries must have been in his early fifties, though he looked younger. He was a tall, trim man, although he was broad-shouldered, and he had a good head of hair which was going grey here and there. He had a friendly, oval face, with steely blue eyes and he wore a well-cut business suit, an expensive looking silk tie over a well-ironed shirt, and stout leather brogues.

"Thanks for seeing me, Mr Humphries. This is a sad time. I'm sorry for your loss."

"Thank you, Detective. Yes, I suppose it is, though Mum had a good innings, and she wouldn't have wanted to linger on deteriorating into infirmity. She was a proud woman," Humphries said, the memory of his mother causing him to tear up a little.

"You said you were going to call us. May I ask why?" Moore said.

"Well, it's just the suddenness of it all. I visited Mum on alternate days with my brother, Dylan. He's a good bit younger than me, but we both liked to see her every two days and make sure she had everything she needed and was being well looked after."

"And when did you see your mother last, Mr Humphries?"

"Yesterday. I popped in on the way home from work. My office is in Blackrock, but I live in Killiney, so it's more or less on the way home."

"What time would that have been?" Moore said.

"Let me see – I left the office at just after six, so about half past, I'd say. She was in the day room with most of the others watching TV."

"And how long did you stay?"

"Not long. I didn't want to interrupt them. I asked her if she needed anything or if there was anything I could do for her, but she said no. So, I stayed about ten minutes and left. I don't like to disturb their routine too much. But at the weekends, when I visit, I often take her out, down to the sea at Bulloch Harbour, or we go for a drive and a walk. She was quite fit, you know."

"So, when you were informed of her sudden death, you felt it was suspicious then?"

"Yes. Don't you?"

"Our investigation is at a very early stage, Mr Humphries, but there are certain aspects of your mother's passing that we are looking into. That's all I can say for now. May I ask, are you married?"

"Yes, indeed I am. Wife and three kids, although they are grown up now. Funny how we still think of them as kids, isn't it?" Humphries said.

"And do any of them ever visit your mother?"

"Occasionally. You know what young people are like – busy, busy, no time for anything. But yes, they did visit her on special occasions – her birthday, Mother's Day, Christmas, Easter, that sort of thing."

"And what does your brother do? Dylan, isn't it?"

"Yes, that's right. Dylan is the black sheep. He's sort of into the arts world. He paints, and writes poetry, but not very successfully. But he gets by somehow."

"Where does he live?"

"He rents a flat in Blackrock, on the seafront. He calls it his studio. I'm sure Mother was paying the rent. Nothing was said, but I'd say that was the arrangement. She may have been giving him more money too. I'm not sure."

"Is that a problem for you?" Moore said.

"No, not at all. It's her money, she can do what she likes with it. My business provides all I need in any case."

"Sorry if this is a bit indelicate, Mr Humphries, but did your mother have much money in her own right?"

"Yes, she did. My father left her well off – he died six years ago – and then she got a good price for her house down in Coliemore Harbour. It was one of those big terraced jobs overlooking the sea. It fetched well over a million when she sold it."

"I presume she left a will?"

"Yes, of course. Everything is divided equally between the three of us as far as I am aware. We have a sister that lives down in Galway, too – Celine."

"Is Celine married?"

"Yes, she is. She's married to a publican, Declan. They run a pub and a restaurant together in Oranmore. It's a popular place. Does very well with the tourists. You might even have heard of it, Sergeant, it's called Brady's."

"No, I'm afraid not, but then I don't know the location at all, except for passing through. Does Celine get to see your mother often?"

"No, rarely. Their pub is very busy and they like to be there anytime it's open to keep an eye on the place, so they don't get up to Dublin much," Humphries said.

"I see. And what about your business, Mr Humphries. How is that doing?"

"Very well, thank you. We have a solid core of ordinary insurance for houses, pubs, shops, industrial clients and a bit of motor. I leave that mostly to my partner, Derek, to deal with. I focus on the event insurance. It's pretty lucrative if you get it right – and I do – well, most of the time, anyway."

"Yes, I saw that on your website. Isn't that a bit risky?"

"How do you mean?" Humphries said.

"Insuring against the weather – that sort of thing?"

"It's not just the weather. Say you have a concert booked for the Aviva Stadium and for some reason or other the band cancels a few days before the event. The organiser clearly has to refund the ticket costs back to the fans, and then there's the stadium to pay for, security etc. The pay-out can be very large, but then so are the premiums. I re-insure much of the risk to make certain I don't come a cropper, but there's still plenty left when all is said and done. But listen, Sergeant, shouldn't you be looking into whatever happened at Cedar Hill?"

"Yes, of course, and we are. There are several officers investigating to see if there was anything amiss. Don't worry, Mr Humphries, if there's been anything fishy going on, we'll get to the bottom of it. Now, if you could just give me the contact details for your brother, I'll be on my way."

Humphries sent Moore an electronic business card to her phone with Dylan's mobile number and email address.

She thanked the man for his time, and left the hotel to go back to the Garda station.

* * *

When she got back to Store Street, Moore asked Séan O'Reilly to take the list of employees from Cedar Hill and check them all out on the Garda PULSE system, as well as the Immigration Department's computers to see if anything of interest popped up. Séan was a civilian worker attached to the detective unit who helped with administrative duties, and could do a lot of the donkey work associated with an investigation when the Gardaí themselves were under pressure. He was young, but very enthusiastic, and seemed to have an insatiable appetite for work which was very handy with Inspector Aidan Burke away.

Moore turned her attention to research using her own PC. She trawled through all the references Google could produce on Stuart Humphries, his business, and his brother, Dylan. There were a few references to Stuart's business scattered here and there among various publication, notably Business Affairs – an online publication about businesses in Ireland. Stuart was featured having paid out large amounts of money when some open-air events had been cancelled, but he had made the most of the publicity, with quotes telling any interested reader that his insurance policies always came good when they were called upon to do so.

Moore went onto a couple of information websites too, and harvested a small amount of detail about Humphries' company accounts. But as his business was not a limited liability firm, there was not much to be had. From what she could gather though, the business appeared to be in reasonably good shape, with a surprisingly large gross income figure.

Dylan Humphries' story was very different. It looked as if he was rather an unsuccessful artist that had tried his hand at many different ventures, but succeeded at none. Some years ago, he had formed a theatre company putting on very unorthodox versions of some of the classic plays from Harold Pinter, Tom Stoppard and even the great Samuel Beckett, but these had generally been poorly reviewed and the company had disbanded after what looked to have been a difficult eighteen months.

Dylan had then declared himself to be a poet, but again struggled to gain any traction in that arena. Finally, he had turned his hand to painting. His work was abstract in nature and left Moore cold. She could see no merit in it at all, and from the reports of the critics, she wasn't alone.

Moore called Dónal Lawler over.

"Dónal, I'd like you to interview Dylan Humphries. To be honest, I doubt if he's a real suspect, but best to nip out and have a chat with him just in case."

"OK, boss. See you later."

Chapter Six

The following day a member of the forensic team that had been out at the old folks' home called Moore.

"Hi, Fiona. We got a few bits and pieces from Mrs Humphries' room that might be of interest. Is it OK if I pop over?"

Moore recognised the voice of Declan Lowry. Moore had worked with him before, and she was impressed with his dedication and energy. He was young; probably in his early thirties, she thought, so much the same age as herself. He had dark hair with a swarthy complexion, and nearly always wore black-rimmed glasses that made him look quite studious. Moore had often seen him togged out in a white scene-of-crime suit, which added to his professorial appearance.

He arrived fifteen minutes later carrying a large plastic evidence bag. Moore brought him into Aidan Burke's office where the two of them sat down.

"Thanks for coming over, Declan. What have you got?" Moore said.

Lowry donned a fresh pair of vinyl gloves and opened the evidence bag.

"Mostly, just the usual bits and pieces. But there was a drawer in the wardrobe that had a will folded away. I have it here," he said, taking out a legal looking document typed on cream vellum paper, with a pink ribbon running down the edge. It was folded length-ways in the manner that many legal documents are.

Moore put on her own pair of gloves and took the will from Lowry. She studied the contents for a moment.

"Interesting. Her son told me that her money was all to be divided between her three children equally, but that's not what it says here. She's left €25,000 each to the two nurses, €10,000 to Cancer Research Ireland and the balance is divided between the children. I wonder how much she actually had."

Lowry reached into the evidence bag again and pulled out a sheaf of what were clearly bank statements.

"These might help," he said, handing the papers to Moore.

Moore studied the National Bank statements and saw that the woman had a balance of €1.8 million. There were regular payments of €5,000 made to the retirement home, another regular payment of €750, which Moore guessed was probably Dylan's rent, along with a few other incidental amounts. There were also some bigger payments made from the account at various irregular intervals. These were of the order of ten or twelve thousand euro at a time, and the money was transferred electronically. Money coming into the account was made up of the woman's state pension of just over €200 a week, and a monthly payment from a private pension provider of €1,735 a month.

Moore took to her jotter and started doing some calculations. After a few minutes, she looked up.

"Well, I'm no actuary, but I reckon her pension pot must be worth around €420,000. Add that to her bank balance, deduct the bequests to the staff, divide by three, and take away the tax and you're left with a cool four hundred grand, or thereabouts, for each of the three children. Pretty good, eh?" Moore said.

"Dead right! Oh, and there's more."

Lowry reached back into the evidence bag and retrieved another much smaller plastic bag and handed it over.

Moore took it and looked quizzically at the item.

"What am I looking at, Declan?"

"We found it under the bed. It's a used phial of morphine."

"Christ, you're such a tease. You could have told me that first!"

"That would have spoiled my grand reveal, Fiona."

"Any prints?" Moore said.

"No, 'fraid not. But I guess that confirms Dr O'Higgins' theory that she was knocked out before she was suffocated."

"Yes, Declan, I guess it does. So that gives us means and opportunity, but not really motive," Moore said.

"What about the money?"

"Maybe, but that needs to be proven. And anyway, who? Twenty-five grand is a lot to a nurse, but not as much as four hundred grand is to a destitute poet!"

"Over to you then," Lowry said, getting up to leave.

"Yeah, I guess. Thanks for coming over, anyway. This is all good stuff."

* * *

Moore went and got herself a cup of coffee, and then sat back behind Aidan Burke's desk looking at the evidence that Lowry had brought in for inspiration. None came.

"Damn it, Burke, why did you have to choose these two weeks to be away!" she said to no one in particular. After a few minutes during which no new ideas came to her, she went in search of Dónal Lawler, whom she found at his desk in the open plan office.

"Right, Dónal, we need to get Mrs Phillips in for a chat. Declan has brought us some new information and we need to talk to her. Can you give her a call, and see if she'll come in voluntarily this afternoon? If not, take a couple of uniformed officers out and bring her in – no excuses. OK?"

"Yes, sure boss. What new information did Lowry have?"

"I'll tell you later, and by the way, did you talk to Dylan Humphries?"

"Yes, I did. I can't see it, boss. He's just not well enough organised to arrange it, and besides he has an alibi. He was with a girl all night. I checked and she confirmed it."

* * *

Marjorie Phillips wasn't at all happy.

"This is outrageous! I have a home to run, and anyway what is it that you think I have done? You can't just demand my presence like this, you really can't!"

Moore let her rant on for a few minutes. She knew the score. The woman would huff and puff about her rights and the injustice of it all until she had run out of steam, then maybe – just maybe – she would catch herself on and start actually helping.

"The reason you are here, Mrs Phillips, is that it has now been confirmed that Mrs Humphries was murdered in your retirement home. She was injected with a dose of morphine, and then suffocated for good measure. We need your help to bring the perpetrator of this callous crime to justice. Now, are you prepared to answer some questions for us?"

Phillips looked even more distraught at this news.

"Yes, yes of course. But I don't see how I can help. Who would do such a terrible thing? That poor woman never harmed anyone," she said, dabbing her nose with a tissue. She went on, "I hope you're not suggesting it had anything to do with me or my staff, Sergeant?"

"I'm not suggesting anything, Mrs Phillips, but let's face it, it happened on your property, and while the woman was in your care," Moore said.

"Oh, this is just too much. Nothing like this has ever happened at Cedar Hill before. It could ruin us."

"Mrs Phillips, we have observed that there is virtually no security at all at Cedar Hill. The front door appears to be open most of the time, the reception desk is rarely occupied, and the CCTV system is inoperative. How do you control who comes in and out?"

"We've never had any trouble, Sergeant. We get deliveries, and there's the laundry service that comes and goes, the doctors, cleaners and so on. And then our residents have visitors – well most of them do – from time to time, but we've never had any difficulty."

"Have any of the residents reported pilfering or anything?"

Phillips squirmed a little in her seat and looked down.

"Occasionally. But mostly it's just that they have forgotten where they have put something, or perhaps they've given something away to a loved one as a gift and don't remember."

"What sort of things?" Moore said.

"Jewellery, watches, rings – that sort of thing. But there's always a rational explanation in the end."

Moore decided to move on, but made a mental note to investigate what may well have been a spate of petty thefts at the home from some of the vulnerable old folks.

"We believe that Mrs Humphries was killed quite late at night. Perhaps around ten-thirty or eleven. Who would be on the premises at that time, Mrs Phillips?"

"Just the night porter and the nurse. I usually go home between six and seven. By that time the catering is finished with and the doctors have been and gone, and everyone is settling down to read or watch TV. Then, at around nine-thirty they start going up to bed. Everyone is usually tucked up for the night by ten-thirty, and the nurse does her rounds to see that they are all comfortable. Older people like a routine, you see."

"What about the porter? Where does he base himself?"

"He has no fixed position, but he often sits at the desk in reception and does a walkabout every now and then during the night. We lock the outer doors soon after nine o'clock, and then he's free to wander around."

"Are there many other ways in and out of Cedar Hill?"

"There's a back entrance we use for certain deliveries. And there's a little kitchenette in the basement used by the groundsman. There's a door through into the lower part of the building from there. But the kitchenette is locked when the groundsman goes home at six."

"Very well, Mrs Phillips. I'll need a full list of all your staff – casuals and all. And I'd like the names of the main suppliers too. You know, the delivery firms and laundry you mentioned. And before you go, have you any idea – even the slightest inkling – who might be behind this?"

"No, officer. I have no idea whatever. It's terrible. Terrible. I'll never get over this."

Chapter Seven

When Mrs Phillips had written out the list for Moore and left the station, Moore passed the information on to Séan O'Reilly and asked him to check up every name on the list. She instructed him to call the laundry company and get the name of the driver who looked after Cedar Hill and include him as well.

"What am I looking for, boss?" O'Reilly said.

"Any criminal records. In fact, anything dodgy at all. See how long they have been working for the companies, and if you find anything, go for known associates as well."

As she was walking away, Dónal Lawler called her.

"Got a sec, Sarge?"

"Sure – what's up?"

"I've been doing a bit more digging into the family. Looks like Stuart has another business he didn't tell us about."

"Really? Do tell!"

"Yeah, Humphries Risk Management Limited. It's registered in the Isle of Man. It's a bit hard to get much information about it, but it looks like it might be in debt."

"Interesting. How much does it owe, and to whom?" Moore said.

"I'm still digging, but it could be quite a bit – maybe as much as two million."

"Wow! Who does he owe it to?"

"Looks like a couple of the Names at Lloyds."

"Who?"

"Lloyds is the big insurance syndicate in London, and the people that run it are apparently called 'Names'– but there's very little information."

"OK, keep digging. Get as much info as you can, and let me know."

There was little more she could do at the station that evening, so Moore decided to call it a day. She had set a number of tasks in motion, and until something new was discovered, the investigation was stuck. Once again, she was feeling that if her boss DI Burke had been around, things might have gone in a different direction, or that they would be further along. It was very frustrating.

When she got home, she cooked herself a light meal of fish from the freezer, pasta and salad, washed down with a modest glass of pinot grigio. When she had cleared away, she sat down with her own PC and rummaged around for a while, but nothing new came to her and after an hour or so she realised she was getting nowhere. She contemplated calling Burke in France, but decided against it. It wasn't fair to disturb his holiday, and in any case, what would he be able to do from over there?

The television did little to improve matters, and by ten o'clock the frustration got too much for her and she packed up and went to bed, hoping that sleep wouldn't elude her.

She had only been asleep for a little over an hour, when the mobile phone on top of her bedside locker started to jangle.

"Sergeant Moore? It's Danny here from the station. There's been another sudden death out at a nursing home in Rathgar. The first responders have heard about the

Glenageary thing, and they have requested that you attend."

"Thanks, Danny. Text me the details. Tell them I'm on my way, and get forensics out too. Make sure the scene is preserved, won't you? I'll be there in twenty minutes or so."

* * *

Dartry Manor was just about as different from Cedar Hill as you could imagine. Built on the grounds of an old and long since demolished Georgian pile, the facility was comprised of three rectangular concrete blocks, each being four storeys high. The flat-roofed buildings were arranged as three sides of a square, and in front of the centre one a wide expanse of well-tended grass with a number of flower beds and young trees stood back from the tarmac parking area in front of the central unit.

The buildings were bland and unattractive, but practical and probably quite easy to manage, although the metal fire escapes zig-zagging down the outer walls at each end did nothing for the aesthetics.

Moore parked her car at the front amongst the small collection of police vehicles that had assembled. A uniformed Garda at the front door – an automatic one which annoyingly kept opening and closing due to where the man was standing – took her name and inspected her warrant card. He directed her to the second floor of block B – room B210.

Inside the premises, it was difficult to escape the institutional nature of the place. Long, brightly lit corridors stretched in every direction. The floors which had some form of vinyl covering were spotlessly clean, and a faint smell of disinfectant pervaded the clinical atmosphere.

Signage with green lettering on a pale grey, aluminium background was liberally dispersed indicating the directions to the 'Dining Room', 'Recreation', 'Clinic',

‘Gymnasium’, ‘Library’, ‘Administration’, ‘Pharmacy’ and other essentials required by the elderly residents.

Moore passed a large sign with red letters on a white background mounted on a wall saying ‘Strictly Residents and Visitors only beyond this point’.

As she walked down one of the long corridors following a sign that had directed her to ‘block B’, Moore noticed that the entire area seemed to be well covered with CCTV cameras, discreetly positioned in the ceiling alongside the smoke detectors and small loudspeakers.

“Let’s hope these ones are actually working!” she said to herself. She pushed on through several sets of double doors with wired glass and blue disks screwed into them saying, ‘Fire door. Keep closed.’

When she arrived in the lobby area of block B, there were two stainless steel lifts. Beside the button used to summon them, a warning sign, again in red letters on a white background, advised ‘Do not use the lift in case of evacuation’, with an arrow pointing to the stairwell nearby.

Moore called the cavernous lift, and ascended slowly to floor 2. When the doors opened, more signage directed her to her left where ‘Rooms B200-220’ were apparently located. As she left the lift, she could see and hear the hub-bub coming from a room that faced out to the front of the building which would have had a pleasant aspect out over the grounds.

The room in which the corpse of the elderly occupant was to be found was surprisingly cheerful. There were fresh flowers on the dresser, and a small collection of black and white family photographs on the walls, some of which looked as if they dated from the 1950s and 1960s. It was spacious, with a bed, a fresh two-seater couch, another comfy chair and a bedside locker, again with a small vase of fresh flowers upon it.

Dr Malcolm O’Higgins was bending over the body of a white-haired woman, lying on her back in the bed. She had a floral twill nightgown on, and Moore noticed a very expensive diamond ring on her left hand. There were two other forensic officers clad in white suits dusting the room for fingerprints, and collecting items from the drawers and wardrobe.

Moore donned plastic overshoes and gloves before entering and speaking to the doctor.

"Evening, Doc. What have you got?"

"Oh, hello Fiona. Meet Mrs Edel Roberts, late of this parish. Eighty-seven years old, and in rude health until this evening, when someone decided that her life should be terminated abruptly."

"Cripes – are you sure?"

O'Higgins straightened up and gave Moore a cold stare, before giving it up and smiling slowly.

"This time, we have the advantage of hindsight, as it were. This is a mirror image of what happened in Glenageary. Same recipe – same outcome. I'll wager we'll find morphine in her veins, and I'm fairly sure she has been suffocated just like poor Mrs Humphries. I'll have a full report after the PM tomorrow."

"OK. Who's in charge here?"

"There's a chargehand – a nurse, or sister or something. She was very distressed. Your guy, Lawler, has taken her downstairs to the kitchens to get her a hot sugary drink."

"Thanks."

Before she went in search of her colleague, she spoke to the lead forensic officer, Phil.

"Make sure we secure all the CCTV. That's the corridors, the entrance, the lobby, outside, and obviously the fire escapes too."

"Right boss. There's not much here, like prints or anything, so we'll be finishing up shortly. I'll make sure the CCTV material is dropped off for you," the young man said.

"Thanks," Moore said.

* * *

Sister Bernie O'Dea was seated with Dónal Lawler in the otherwise empty dining room with a mug of strong tea, half consumed, in front of her.

Lawler made the introductions, and Moore sat down beside him, facing the girl. O'Dea appeared to be in her early thirties, of slim build with a ruddy complexion and short wavy brown hair. She was dressed in the standard nurse's uniform – a blue button-through dress, a white over-apron all held in against her body with a thick, elasticated black belt. A small fob watch was suspended, upside down, from the top left-hand corner of her tunic.

"This is a dreadful business, Sister. May I ask who found the woman?" Moore said.

"I did. I was doing my rounds – just to make sure everyone was settled down for the night – and as I passed Mrs Roberts' room, I heard a radio playing. It was tuned to a pop station, which isn't like her at all. She usually listens to classical music on Lyric FM. So, I knocked on the door, and when there was no reply, I went in. I assumed she was just asleep, but when I took a closer look, I could see her pallor wasn't right. I felt for a pulse, and then… well, you know."

O'Dea put a tissue up to her nose and sniffed.

"What time would that have been?" Moore said.

"It was just after eleven."

"I don't wish to be indelicate, Sister, but surely quite a few of your residents pass away?" Moore said.

"You'd be surprised, Sergeant. Of course, it happens, but quite rarely. They mostly get something and are transferred to an acute hospital before the end. And Mrs Roberts was so full of life. I certainly wasn't expecting her to die," O'Dea said, with the emphasis on the word 'her'.

"I see. She was in good health, then?"

"Yes, very. The only reason she was in here is that she had had a stroke – a very mild one – and she was living on her own, so her family thought it best that she be properly looked after."

"How long has she been here?" Lawler said.

"I'd have to check the records to be accurate, but from memory, I think just over a year."

"And how long have you worked here, Sister?" Moore said.

"Nearly four years now. I've always been a geriatric nurse, but the conditions and pay here are better than in the hospital system, so I left the HSE and came to Dartry Manor."

"Is the place well run?" Moore said.

"Yes, very. The O'Sullivans are very particular. Our staffing levels are actually higher than the requirements dictate, and the place is immaculately maintained. We always get anything we need to make the residents more comfortable."

"How many staff are on tonight?" Lawler said.

"There will be seven of us plus the security man. That's two nurses for each block, and I supervise."

"What are the names of the nurses looking after block B?" Moore said.

"That's Jacintha and Ilyana. They are both Eastern European. Lovely girls."

Moore nodded to Dónal who got up and went in search of the two nurses.

"Have you been in touch with the O'Sullivans?" Moore said.

"No. Not yet. I suppose I should call them. What do you think happened?"

"It's OK. I'll call them if you'd prefer. Just get me a number – it might be better coming from me."

"OK. Thanks, I'd prefer that. Look, I'd better go and see that everyone else is all right. Do you need me for anything more just now?"

"No, you're fine. We can talk later. What time do you finish up?"

"Six o'clock."

"OK. I'll come and find you then."

Chapter Eight

The man parked the car some two hundred yards short of the bungalow he had come to see. It was early afternoon on a bright, sunny day, and after locking the car, he strolled up along the road till he came to the house he wished to investigate. The place was in quite poor condition, with an overgrown front garden, and rusty iron gates that looked as if they could no longer be closed due to the build-up of weeds on the gravel driveway. The paintwork that could be seen from the road was tired and weathered by the sun, and in the bay window to the right of the front door, dirty net curtains hung loosely down.

The man, who was a mere five foot six inches tall with only a very short crop of hair which simply refused to grow any longer, walked into the garden of the house and started looking curiously around.

Next door, in the front garden of the next bungalow, an elderly man with thinning white hair dressed in beige twill trousers and a maroon jumper was tending to the immaculately manicured garden. He had clearly just mown the grass, which was displaying a pronounced striped pattern, and he was now trimming the edges of the lawn where it met the flower beds with some gadget or other.

The man greeted the gardener. "You have that looking amazing, sir. It's quite a contrast to this one, if I may say."

The gardener stood up, pleased to have some social interaction, and of course, equally pleased to have his work praised in such a manner.

"Well, I do my best. I like to keep it nice."

"What's the story here?" the man asked, nodding towards the estate agent's signboard stuck into the ground against the front garden wall of the fixer-upper.

"That's poor Miss Finnucane's place. It's a shame to see it in that condition, but she couldn't manage it anymore, you see."

"Oh, I see. Did she... well... you know?"

"Oh, no. She became a bit disorientated, so her niece decided she would be better off going into a home where she could be properly looked after. She works in insurance in town somewhere – the niece, I mean. They moved her to a very nice place over near Dalkey. She'll be well minded there. She was inclined to go out walking and not be able to find her way back. I retrieved her more than once in a bewildered state down near the station."

"Ah, right. Miss Finnucane, did you say?"

"Yes, that's right, Maeve Finnucane. She's lived here for, oh, let me see, it must be more than thirty years. She used to be a primary school teacher in Dún Laoghaire. Are you interested in the house? Sorry, I didn't catch your name," the neighbour said.

"Maybe. I buy some of these old places in poor condition and restore them to their former glory, and then sell them on. But this one might be a bit out of my range, pricewise. Have you any idea how much they're asking?"

"No, sorry. But you can look it up on the net or give the agent a call. She's a nice young girl. She'll give you all the details. We'll miss Maeve of course, but it will be nice to have the place overhauled. It's giving the road a bit of an uncared for look the way it is."

"Right, I'll do that. What did you say was the name of the place where they put Miss Finnucane?"

The gardener scratched his head and looked into the middle distance for a moment.

"Eh, Vico... Vico, wait now, Vico View – yes that's it. It's on the Vico Road. Lovely spot. Very select, or so I've heard."

"Well, thanks for that. I'll be on my way now. I'll give the agent a ring as you suggested. Keep up the good work!"

The gardener raised his hand in a salute.

"Bye now. May see you again if you come to view the old place." He returned to his toil, clipping the edges of the grass with long-handled shears.

The man reckoned that with the niece at work in town, Miss Finnucane would be unlikely to have visitors in the middle of the afternoon. He got back to his car, and looked up Vico View on the sat nav.

"That's handy. It's only about ten minutes away," he said to himself, starting the car.

* * *

Vico View occupied a stunning position overlooking Killiney Bay on the high side of the Vico Road in Dalkey. It was a large black and white double-fronted Victorian house, that had been extended significantly to the rear. The house was approached by a steep driveway, with a circle of tarred parking in front. There was just one other car present – an expensive looking silver Mercedes.

He got out of his ten-year-old Nissan, and went into the building, finding the front door open. Inside, the place was tastefully decorated, with a plush navy carpet on the hall floor, and pictures with scenic views of the surroundings arranged along the walls in gilt frames above the dado rail. A girl in her late twenties sat behind a semi-circular mahogany reception desk furnished with a swan-necked lamp, a PC and a phone. A badge fixed to the front of her uniform told anyone who was interested that her name was Anna.

"Hello, Anna. I've come to see Miss Finnucane. I'm her nephew, Jeremy," the man said, clutching the small box of expensive chocolates he had purchased in Dalkey Village on his way over from the old woman's house.

"Oh, right. She'll be in the day room," Anna said getting up from her desk. "Here, I'll show you," she said, smiling warmly at the imposter.

The day room was warm – a little too much so for the man's liking – but he understood that old people can get quite cold. Inside, three people sat in different comfortable chairs. Fortunately for the man, the other two residents were male, so the white-haired woman sitting in the window staring blankly out across the gardens to sea, had to be Maeve Finnucane.

"Now, Miss Finnucane. Jeremy is here to see you, isn't that nice?" Anna said, positioning a visitor's chair near to the woman. The elderly spinster looked blankly at the man for a moment and then returned her gaze to the view out through the window without saying anything.

"Hello, Aunt Maeve. Look, I've brought you some chocolates. They're your favourites."

Anna leant in close to the man and whispered, "She's having one of her off days today. I'm sorry – she gets like this sometimes. I doubt if she even recognises you."

The man gave Anna a knowing smile, indicating that he understood.

He pretended to engage Miss Finnucane in some banal conversation about the lovely place and the nice day, but thankfully, the woman was out of it. After a few minutes of completely one-sided conversation, the man got up and went back out to the front desk.

"Thanks, Anna. She's not very talkative today, just as you said. I'll just leave these up in her room for her. She may be feeling better later on. Which is her room?"

"Oh, I can do that for you, Jeremy. It's no trouble."

"No, I'd like to see where she sleeps anyway. I haven't been here before, you see."

"Oh, very well. Up the stairs, second door on the left. It's number 12. It should be open."

"Thanks."

He trotted up the stairs. As the man went up to room 12, he took careful note of the layout of the home. He spotted the usual accoutrements – the fire alarm, the smoke detectors, the CO detectors and the fire extinguishers, but could see no CCTV on the upper floor. In fact, the only sign of a camera had been at the front door.

The man left the chocolates in room 12 on the bedside locker. He examined the room. It was quite sparsely furnished, though it looked very comfortable and had a nice view out across the front garden to the sea beyond. When he had finished a cursory exploration, he left and went to the end of the upstairs corridor to study the fire escape arrangements. As usual, there was an exterior stair fitted to the outside of the building, with what looked like an alarmed door leading out onto it. Over the door a green sign showing an image of a running person and the word EXIT in large green letters indicated the purpose of the escape. There were four other guest rooms off the landing.

He made his way back downstairs. Before departing, he peeked back into the day room and waved cheekily to Miss Finnucane who hadn't moved from her chair. She was still looking out to sea with a vacant expression on her face.

"Thanks, Anna. See you again shortly," he said with a smile, and left.

Chapter Nine

Moore had gone to get a few hours' sleep before driving back to Dartry Manor to speak to Sister O'Dea before she went off duty. When she pulled up to the door, she noticed that there was a sleek BMW 7 Series parked in front of the building, which, she assumed, belonged to the owners.

The front door was locked, but Moore could see that there was someone inside, so she tapped gently on the glass so as not to disturb the peace of the place. The door buzzed, and Moore went inside to find a stout woman in her mid-fifties with short curly grey hair and a stern face sitting at the reception desk.

"Police, I take it," the woman said rather sourly, in a pronounced country accent.

"Detective Sergeant Fiona Moore," she said extending her warrant card, which was carefully scrutinized by the woman, "and you are?"

"Dympna O'Sullivan. I'm the proprietor. This is a terrible business. Bernie tells me you think poor Mrs Roberts may have been killed. That's hardly likely, now is it, Sergeant? Surely she just passed away in her sleep?"

"Obviously, we are still investigating. But we do suspect she was killed, yes. And you should know that there was another old lady who met a very similar fate in a nursing home not too far away from here recently."

"Oh, dear God, what's the world coming to?" Mrs O'Sullivan said.

"I was hoping to have another word with Bernie before she went off. Is she still here?"

"No, no, she's not. She was very distraught, poor girl. I sent her home when I got here at half past two, after I'd poured a stiff brandy into her."

"Oh, OK. Looks like I've had a wasted journey then. But seeing as I'm here, do you think you could get me a list of all your employees with their addresses and Social Security numbers? That's everyone – outdoor staff as well. And I'll need a list of your suppliers too. Anyone that calls frequently to the place. Do you keep a visitors' book?"

"Well, we do, but regular visitors – close relatives and the like – don't always sign in, and we don't like to demand it," Mrs O'Sullivan said.

"So, basically, you have no idea who's in or out much of the time?" Moore said.

"We don't need to, Sergeant. We've never had any strays wandering around here. It's too out of the way. And we have CCTV on the main door and the corridors anyway. I understand your forensic people have taken the films away."

"Did Mrs Roberts have any relatives or friends that called on her?"

"No, I'm afraid not. I don't think she had anyone at all. We get a few like that every year. Her husband died some time ago, and as far as I know they had no children, so she was pretty much all alone in the world. But I'll check with the girls and see if she had any visitors other than family."

"I see," Moore said somewhat frostily. She wasn't warming to Mrs O'Sullivan.

"Very well. Perhaps you could forward the list on to me later this morning," Moore said, giving the woman her card. "My email address is on this."

* * *

There was nothing more she could do at the home, so Moore went back into town to the Garda station in Store Street. When she got in, she went upstairs to the open plan and started to update the whiteboard with details of the new victim.

By the time she had done that, and put all the new information into the Garda PULSE system, some of the others were starting to arrive at the station.

Moore brought Dónal Lawler up to speed on developments.

"Jesus, boss. Does this mean we have a serial killer on our hands?"

"Not yet, and I don't want any rumours like that going around. But it's clear the M. O. is much the same in both cases, so you never know," Moore said.

"What are you going to do, boss?"

"What *we're* going to do, Dónal, is catch the bugger. Right?"

"Yes, of course. But how?"

"Start by seeing if there are any possible links between the two cases – apart from the obvious, that is. You know – any suppliers that the two homes might have in common, like launderers, caterers, cleaning companies, landscape firms – anything at all. Then look at any staff that may have worked at both places. We need to see if there's any possible connection there, however tenuous. Did the first victim have a mobile phone, do you know?"

"I don't think so. I'll check, but I don't think they found one. Is it important?"

"Could be."

"Look, I'm going to need help with all this cross-referencing. Séan is good, but he's not Superman. Can we get some more people to help us out?" Lawler said.

"I'm going to see the Super as soon as he's in and request more manpower. It's a damn shame that the DI isn't here," Moore said.

"How much more holidays has he got?"

"Another week. Trust him to be away when all this kicks off. Typical!"

Moore sat at her desk trying to figure out the best way to approach Superintendent Heffernan. He was generally supportive, but always had at least one eye on the political aspect of what was going on, and he wouldn't like this – not one little bit. She knew it was only a matter of hours before the press got hold of it, and then all hell would break loose. She was just finalising her strategy, when her phone rang.

"Moore."

"Hello, Sergeant. It's Maureen here from upstairs. Superintendent Heffernan would like to see you as soon as possible."

"Right, Maureen. I'll be up directly."

When Fiona Moore answered the summons from within and entered Heffernan's office, it was immediately clear that this wasn't going to go well. Heffernan wasn't alone. Seated in front of his desk was none other than the Assistant Commissioner, dressed in full regalia and looking grim.

"Come in, Detective Sergeant. I think you know the Assistant Commissioner. Take a seat."

"Yes, good morning, sir," she said addressing the man, who simply nodded without making any reply.

"Sit down, Sergeant. I understand that there has been another sudden death at one of these old folks' homes. What can you tell us about it?"

Moore outlined what they knew so far, but was very puzzled as to how the AC had got wind of the second death so quickly. She decided to go for broke.

"I'm sorry, sir, but may I ask how you got to hear of the death out at Dartry Manor? It only happened during the night."

Heffernan responded, "The Assistant Commissioner's mother is a resident in Dartry Manor, Sergeant, and she phoned him at 7 a.m. this morning with the grim news."

The man was clearly seriously miffed that the AC had got to hear of the incident before he had himself, and Moore knew she would have to tread very carefully from now on.

"Do you think the rest of the residents in either of these facilities are in danger, Sergeant?" the AC said.

"I can't say, sir, but I think probably not. I'm arranging for a notification to be sent to all private nursing homes in the Dublin area later today, advising the operators to tighten security. It's extraordinary how lax it is at some of the homes."

"How close are you to finding out who is behind these attacks, and do you think it is the same person?" Heffernan said.

"It's too early to say, sir. But the investigation is progressing. We may get lucky when the forensics come back from Dartry Manor."

As soon as the words were out of her mouth, Moore realised she had made a mistake.

"Are you saying you are relying on luck, Sergeant?" the AC said.

"No, sir. I meant it as a figure of speech."

Heffernan was keen to ensure that Moore and the AC didn't lock horns – that would do no one any good – so he intervened.

"Right, well, I've put a call in to Inspector Burke. I'm recalling him from his holidays. You need someone senior on this, Sergeant. I'll try and get him back today."

"Do you think that is really necessary, sir?"

"I wouldn't be doing it if I thought it wasn't necessary, Sergeant, would I? Now off you go and see if you can make any progress before we're featuring in all tomorrow's newspapers. I can just see it now, 'Old Bill foxed by Old Folks killings'," he said and drew an imaginary headline with his hand in the air.

Moore was seething. She got up and left without saying goodbye to either man, for fear that she would explode and destroy her career in the doing. She just managed not to slam the door of Heffernan's office on her way out.

Chapter Ten

When Moore got back downstairs she went and fixed herself a strong coffee and took it into Aidan Burke's office to calm herself down. When she had taken a few mouthfuls, she called Dónal Lawler in.

"God, Dónal, this is a total mess. I've just had a right bollocking from Heffernan, and he's only bringing Burke back from his bloody holidays, isn't he?"

She went on to tell Lawler about the connection to the Assistant Commissioner, and the fact that Heffernan was livid that he had been told about the second case by a more senior officer.

"You weren't to know that the AC's mother was a resident in Dartry Manor, boss. It's not your fault."

"Tell that to that lot upstairs! You know how it works – when the shit hits the fan it ultimately travels downwards. Always has, always will."

"Anyway, it will be good to have the DI back with us. We need all the help we can get with this one," Lawler said.

"Yeah, I know. But why does it feel like I've failed miserably?"

"Look, neither of us is bloody Superman or Superwoman. These things have only just happened. It was darn bad luck that the AC's mother happened to be a resident up in Dartry, but that's not our fault either. Let's just do our job. Keep detecting. Keep investigating. You know that's what gets results. Anyway, we have some more information on the first case."

"Oh? What's that?"

"Yer man – Mr Smoothie Humphries, the insurance bloke – well he's only up to his backside in debt, isn't he? That event insurance company that he runs is in trouble. Apparently, he's taken some very big hits arising from the storms last year. Several of the gigs he had insured were cancelled with all the bad weather we had, and he had to pay out millions," Lawler said.

"But I thought he told us that he laid all the risk off with Lloyds or something?"

"He did, but he didn't, if you see what I mean. He carried enough of it to put him properly in the red. His fancy house is re-mortgaged up to the hilt, and the bank has taken away his debit card and cheque book."

"Wow. And now he's likely to inherit a large fortune. Handy, eh?" Moore said.

"Just what I was thinking."

Séan O'Reilly appeared in the doorway of the office and said, "Excuse me, Sergeant, I have been looking at the CCTV from Dartry Manor like you asked me to, and I think I've spotted something."

"Great. C'mon, Dónal, let's go have a look-see," Moore said.

* * *

The three of them made their way out to the open plan where O'Reilly had rigged a PC up to a large screen. When they were all seated in front of it, O'Reilly clicked a few keys on the PC's keyboard and a view of the upstairs corridor of block B at Dartry Manor came into view.

"It's only low resolution video, but it's pretty clear all the same, and as you can see it's time and date stamped," O'Reilly said.

The screen showed the empty corridor with the even numbered rooms on the left and the odd numbered ones on the right. There were eight rooms on each side, and room B210 was about halfway along. They waited patiently for something to happen.

Sensing the detectives' impatience, O'Reilly said, "It's just coming up now at 10:28. Watch."

Sure enough, as the scrolling time stamp rolled past 10:28 a nurse appeared with her back to the camera walking down along the corridor. She went directly to room B210 and entered without knocking. The film kept going, and three minutes later the door to the room opened again, and the nurse came back out. She was careful not to show her face to the camera, and walked away and around the corner at the end of the corridor into a vestibule that acted as a seating area, and led to the fire escape.

"Looks like Sister O'Dea, though it's a bit hard to tell," Moore said.

"Yes, but didn't she say she went into Roberts' room at around eleven? This is half an hour earlier," Lawler said.

"There's something else," O'Reilly said.

"What?" Moore said.

"I'll rewind it and run that bit again. Have a close look at the nurse's feet as she comes back out of the room," O'Reilly said.

He rewound the DVD, making it look as if Sister O'Dea was walking backwards like an old black and white cartoon, and stopped it just as she was emerging from the victim's room. He wound it on again for a second or two and stopped the film just as the nurse was coming out onto the corridor.

"Have a look at her feet," O'Reilly said.

"Crikey! I see what you mean. They must be size 9 or more. Or is it some form of distortion from the video camera?" Moore said.

"I don't think so. And they are men's outdoor shoes in any case. Not the kind of thing a nurse would wear around the home. I think there's a good chance that this isn't nurse O'Dea at all," O'Reilly said.

"You know, I think you could be right. Wow! Well done, Séan. But just to be sure, why don't you call Sister O'Dea, Dónal, and check out what kind of footwear she uses when she's on duty. And while you're at it, ask her again about the time she went into Mrs Roberts' room when she heard the radio," Moore said.

* * *

Dónal Lawler was back a few minutes later.

"Right. O'Dea says that it was definitely just before eleven when she went upstairs to check on things and heard the radio going in Roberts' room. She remembers because when she went in, the eleven o'clock news was being broadcast on the pop station that the radio was tuned to. And she confirmed that she wears lightweight trainers when she's at work in the home. Nothing like the shoes we saw on the film. And finally, I got Séan to run the CCTV footage forward, and we can see her going into the room at 10:59 on the video, so that shows that the timestamp is pretty accurate too."

"Excellent. This is our first big breakthrough. Go and have another look at the CCTV footage. See if you can get a glimpse of the imposter's face at all. Check to see if there's any reflective surfaces anywhere. It was dark outside, so a window would act like a mirror. That would give us a look at her or him," Moore said.

Moore walked over to the whiteboard and drew a circle in red, and a connecting line to the photograph of Mrs Roberts. Inside the circle she wrote the single word 'suspect?' and stood back.

Dónal Lawler came over to her as she stood back and studied the meagre information on the board.

"If only we could connect the intruder to the other home in Glenageary. Then we'd be more or less certain that this is our man," Moore said.

"Why don't I see if there's any more CCTV in the area of Dartry Manor – like out on the road or something? If we could see someone leaving the premises either on foot or in a car at, say, 10:35, then that could be worth following up. What do you think?"

"Good idea. At least it will give us something to show the DI we haven't been sitting around drinking coffee!" Moore said.

Chapter Eleven

Moore made sure that she was in work early the following day. She needed to get there before Burke arrived. She's been at her desk for about twenty minutes when he turned up.

"Hello, sir. Welcome back!" she said as he walked into the office. The DI was looking well, with a healthy suntan. He was dressed casually in smart, pale-coloured chinos and a Lacoste polo shirt, worn under a new-looking leather jacket.

"Thanks a bunch! Give me five minutes and then come in with whatever you've got, will you?"

Burke moved away to his own office.

She gave him time to settle in, and then went into his office.

"How was France?" she said, easing herself into the chair facing Burke a few minutes later.

"Short. So, what's going on here that you can't manage without me?"

"What did Heffernan tell you?" Moore asked.

"Very little. He wasn't in a storytelling mood. Just told me to get my ass back here *tout suite* or words to that effect, so here I am!"

Moore spent some time bringing her boss up to date with everything they knew so far. As she went through the meagre evidence, Burke made notes on a jotter. When she had finished, they both remained silent for some time, with Burke tapping his pen on the pad where he had made his notes.

"OK. So, have you checked to see if there is any connection between the two deceased?" Burke said.

"Sorry, how do you mean?"

"Well, they could be sisters or cousins. Or maybe they worked together somewhere in the past, or perhaps they were neighbours. What have you checked?"

"We haven't got around to that yet, but I'll get Séan working on it now."

"It stands to reason they may have something in common, apart from the fact that they were old and in a home. Did Mrs Roberts have any kids, or close relatives?" Burke said.

"We don't think so. The home said not, but it needs to be checked further."

"See if she had a will then, and see what shape her finances were in. Those places aren't cheap."

"Do you think this is about money, sir?" Moore asked.

"It could be – often is. And on that score, I'd be talking to Stuart Humphries again if I were you, based on what you've told me. Tell you what – why don't I have a go at him while you're checking out the other stuff with Dónal?"

"Yeah, OK. I have his business card out on my desk. I'll give it to you. He has offices in Blackrock."

"Have we sent a memo round to all the old folks' homes in the Dublin area?" Burke said.

"Yes, we have."

"Right. Oh, and get forensics back out to Dartry Manor. It looks from the CCTV that chummy probably departed via the fire escape. Get them to look for footprints coming down the metal stairs. There's often some clay or mud on the ground at the bottom of those things where the rain has washed stuff down from the roof. Get them to look for prints on the fire door and the handrail too. You never know, we might get lucky."

"OK, I'll get onto it. Do you think he or she will strike again?"

"You know the pattern with these things. If it's a serial killer then he'll get more and more audacious until he makes a mistake or until we catch him. I'd say it's a certainty."

"Great. Are we done for now then, sir?"

"Yes. Just get me Stuart Humphries' details and we'll have a briefing first thing tomorrow."

"Yes. I'll tell the others."

* * *

As Burke drove out to Blackrock his mind wandered to what his brother and family would be doing in France at this time. The weather had been stupendous while he was there, and every day they had planned some simple adventure to keep the kids occupied. One of the best days had involved an outing to a lake where canoeing was organised. Burke had taken Shane, Cormac's eldest, out in his canoe, and they had splashed around for what seemed like hours. At one stage they challenged Cormac and Aoife, Cormac's daughter, to a race which they won easily, and perhaps a bit unfairly. To compensate, Burke had treated them all to a fabulous lunch at the open-air café that was pitched at the side of the lake. It was one of the best days of the truncated holiday, and Burke wished that he was still there with them in France.

As Burke pulled his car into a space almost directly in front of Humphries Insurance Broker's offices, he reset his brain to tackle the current situation. He had phoned ahead to make sure Humphries would be available to see him, and as he entered the office, the man himself was seated at one of the desks.

With introductions complete, Humphries showed Burke into his own private office at the back of the shop. With coffee offered and declined, the men got down to business.

"I see you operate event insurance, Mr Humphries, is that correct?"

"Yes, I do. I try to keep it separate from the main business here. It's very different, you see."

"Our information shows that you have suffered some pretty heavy losses recently in that side of things. You are pretty deep in debt."

Humphries threw back his head and laughed out loud.

"Oh, my dear fellow, you don't know much about this kind of thing, do you? You can't judge performance on one, or even two consecutive years in this business. It waxes and wanes something shocking. One year we can chalk up what appear to be huge losses, and the over the next year or two, more than make up for it. Yes, you are correct. Just now, we are at a low point in the curve, but wait till you see – by this time next year it will have righted itself. If you don't believe me, have a look at my books for the last ten years. On a moving average basis, I clear in excess of three hundred thousand annually."

"I see. And how do you fund your losses during the down-cycle, Mr Humphries?"

"The underwriters at Lloyds know me well. I've been dealing with the same group of Names for years and years. They know the business too, and they have no issue extending my credit line when it's needed. They know they'll get it back and then some sooner or later."

"I think I remember seeing something in the 1990s about Lloyds losing vast amounts over some asbestos thing or other," Burke said.

"Oh yes, we all remember that! Tragic. But if you've looked at it since, it's making very good money again these days. As I said, Inspector, cyclical – very cyclical, and the upside is nearly always more than the downside. Lloyds is over three hundred years old, you know."

"Yes, I suppose. But to get back to your mother's affairs, Mr Humphries. We've seen a few quite large payments going out of her account from time to time over the last year. Sums of ten thousand, twelve thousand, those sorts of amounts. Do you know what that's about?"

Humphries remained silent for a moment.

"Well, I suppose you'll find out in any case. Yes, Inspector, those were to me. You see my bank doesn't really understand the cyclical nature of my business either, and as you know they are very conservative these days regarding loans and overdrafts since the crash. I'm afraid they closed me down a few months back, so I had to ask mother for a sort of dig out. She didn't mind. And there's no reason why that waster Dylan should be the only one to benefit from her wealth," Humphries said, obviously a little embarrassed about the matter.

"Does your sister know about this?"

"Celine – I doubt it. I certainly didn't tell her, and I doubt if mother did. Will she have to know?"

"That's up to you, but if you want to be fair to both her and Dylan, you will factor it in when you're divvying up your mother's estate."

"I suppose. But listen, Inspector, why all the interest in my business affairs. Surely you don't think I could have had anything to do with my mother's death, do you?"

"Our investigation is at an early stage, Mr Humphries, and money is a powerful motive in my experience. But don't worry, I'm not accusing you of anything. Just being thorough."

"I should bloody well hope not! Is there anything else I can help you with?" Humphries said, stiffening his demeanour noticeably.

"Just one more thing, Mr Humphries. Did your mother know a woman by the name of Mrs Roberts? Mrs Edel Roberts from around the Rathgar area."

“I don’t think so. She never mentioned her if she did. Why do you ask?”

“Just loose ends, Mr Humphries. Well, I won’t keep you any longer. Thanks for your time,” Burke said, getting up to leave and extending his arm.

“Don’t mention it,” Humphries said, shaking Burke’s hand, “I’ll see you out.”

Chapter Twelve

The man looked himself up and down in the long mirror on the back of his wardrobe door. He had ironed the blue nurse's uniform carefully before putting it on, and he had combed the wig a number of times to make it look as if the wearer had just come back from the hairdresser.

"That should do nicely," he said to himself as he twisted left and right in the mirror image, "I'm looking forward to this. Number three, and the best one yet!"

He smoothed the front of the uniform down one last time, grabbed the black handbag that he had purchased from the charity shop in Sandymount a few days earlier, and left his dingy flat.

He drove his old silver Nissan out along the Rock Road towards Dalkey. It was nearly 10:25 – that strange time of the night when the roads were really quiet. It was raining a little, and the windscreen wipers on the old car sloshed around making odd whining noises, but doing little to improve his visibility. He had been careful to put enough fuel in the car so that he wouldn't have to stop going out or coming back. Those pesky petrol stations all had CCTV these days.

He arrived in Dalkey Village at 10:50 – perfect.

He drove up to the Vico Road and parked on the left-hand side amongst the string of cars, some of which contained courting couples who were clearly sufficiently occupied with each other to miss seeing him altogether. He crossed over and walked up the steep path to Vico View, dodging around the back before he arrived at the open area in front of the main building.

He was getting soaked, but he was determined to carry his mission through, despite the weather. It wouldn't make any difference in any case, he thought, his disguise would protect him.

At the rear of the main building, he climbed onto the fire escape. The weather was now his accomplice. The heavy cloud cover ensured that the back of the property was more or less in pitch darkness, and although there were halogen lights suspended above the fire escape, they weren't set to come on unless the alarm had been activated. There were no passive infrared detectors fitted.

He climbed the fire escape silently, making sure that there was no one about to see him. When he reached the first-floor landing, he took two magnetic contacts that he had made at home earlier, joined by a long piece of bell wire, and attached them to the door and the frame. He then used an ordinary kitchen knife to slip the locking mechanism on the fire exit open. His heart was thumping as he slowly pulled the door open a fraction, half expecting the alarm to go off, but silence prevailed.

He eased the door open further. He was lucky that there was no wind to whistle down the corridor and announce his presence. When the fire escape door was opened wide enough, he ducked under the wire, and entered the home.

He peeped around the corner of the vestibule that the fire escape opened into and saw that there was no one on the landing. All was quiet. He tip-toed down to room 12 and waited, listening carefully for any sign of movement or stirring within – but there was none.

Working quickly, he took the syringe out of his uniform pocket, slipped off the needle cover, and filled it with morphine from the phial he had in his other hand. He opened the door silently, and went into Miss Finnucane's bedroom.

The old lady was lying on her back with her mouth open, and was clearly asleep. The man moved to the edge of the bed, and gently turned the woman's arm over to expose the underside of her forearm. Her veins stood obligingly through her paper-thin skin, and he easily found the one he wanted. Even as he injected the old woman with the deadly liquid, she barely flinched.

With the woman now in a veritable coma, it only took him another minute to grab one of her pillows and finish the job. When she had breathed her last, he put the pillow back on the armchair beside the bed.

"That'll do you, nasty old bitch," he said softly, looking at the corpse of the woman he had just killed. "It was too good for you!"

He checked around to see that he had left nothing behind, and prepared to leave. Before exiting the room, he found Miss Finnucane's portable radio, tuned it to Sunshine 106, and left it running at a low volume on the dresser.

He left the same way he had come in. He gently closed the fire door at the top of the metal staircase and removed the magnetic contacts and wire that he had brought with him, winding it into a ball and putting it all carefully back into his uniform pocket. He descended the stairs and ducked down through the undergrowth, onto the driveway, and back out onto Vico Road. The rain had set in in earnest by now, and once again he got soaked getting back to his car – but it didn't matter to him – his mission was complete. He got back into the old Nissan and set off back to Ringsend, feeling elated and relieved.

As he passed Blackrock Village, just at the bottom of Mount Merrion Avenue, he encountered a Garda checkpoint.

"Christ – what am I going to do now?" he said to himself, panicking.

"I can't speak to the feckers dressed like this, that's for sure!"

The vehicle three cars in front of him had been stopped, and the young Garda was having an animated chat with the driver. After a few minutes, he signalled the car to pull over to the side, where a colleague was waiting to carry on the conversation.

"Damn, damn, damn!" the man said to himself.

As the car in front passed through the checkpoint, he drew up to where the Guard had his hand outstretched. The Guard shone his torch into the car, but seeing a nurse in uniform, and having checked the tax, insurance and NCT discs in the windscreen, he simply waved the car on.

"Fuck me. That was close," he said as he accelerated away towards the safety of home.

Chapter Thirteen

Marcella Kane pulled her smart, new Mini up outside the shabby bungalow with the 'For Sale' sign displayed in the garden. The elderly gentleman was out in the front garden next door, hunting for any weeds that dared to put in an appearance.

As Kane wrestled with the rusty gate to allow her to enter the property, the old man stood up and waved.

"Hello, Marcella. Nice day. Any interest in the old place?" he said, walking over slowly to the low hedge that divided the two properties and leaning on his hoe.

"I have a viewing this afternoon. I just came up to see that it was looking as well as it could," Kane said.

"Is it that bloke that was round here a few days ago asking about it?"

"No, it's a young couple who are looking for somewhere to do up that's not too expensive. They have a mortgage approved, but they can't afford anywhere swish. Who was the man you were talking about?"

"Just a guy that was poking around. Said he was a builder or something and was always on the lookout for what he called 'fixer-uppers'. I told him to give you a call, and he took your number down from the sign. Was he in touch?"

"No, no he wasn't. Odd. Did you get his name by any chance?" Marcella said.

"No, I'm afraid not. To be honest, he looked a bit shifty. I didn't want to encourage him too much. You never know what people are really at these days. He might have been casing the place – or mine – for all I know."

The estate agent laughed.

"You have a suspicious mind, Mr Harris. Anyway, I best get on. See you later. Your garden looks amazing!"

The man just waved dismissively at the girl and returned to his quest for errant vegetation.

* * *

In Store Street, Burke, mindful of the intervention by the Assistant Commissioner, was keen to move things along as quickly as possible. He summoned the team together in the open plan with the whiteboard bearing pictures of the deceased as a backdrop.

"Right, what have we got, everyone? Have we established a connection between our two victims?" he said, looking at Moore for a reply.

"No, sir. I can't find anything that links them except for the obvious – that is, the way they met their end and the fact that they were both in residential care."

"What about the homes themselves? Anything in common, apart from the fact that they have been the scene of a murder recently? Dónal?"

"I can't see anything, boss. They are very different. Cedar Hill is a small privately-owned outfit, whereas Dartry is a much bigger operation altogether owned by a small consortium led by a Dr O'Sullivan. He's retired from medical practice now, and spends his time looking after the homes. They have two other similar operations too, but Dartry is the biggest."

"What about the staff? Have we interviewed all of them that had any contact with the deceased?" Burke said.

"Yes, sir, and we'll be starting to work on the suppliers today to see if there are any in common."

Just then, Séan O'Reilly came into the room.

"Sir. There's a phone call for you from Dalkey. They say it's urgent."

"Thanks, Séan. Put it through here please."

Burke moved to a desk and picked up the phone.

"Burke," he said.

"Good morning, Inspector. This is Sergeant O'Malley from Dalkey. I thought you might like to know that there's been a sudden unexplained death of an old woman in one of the homes here in the town. Vico View – up on the Vico Road. They called the ambulance at about eight o'clock, but I understand the woman was long gone."

"I see. Have they moved the body?" Burke said.

"No, sir. The ambulance men were aware of the other deaths recently. They attended the one in Glenageary, so they left everything alone and called us."

"Good. OK. We'll be along shortly. Have you called the pathologist?"

"No, sir. I thought I'd leave that to you."

"OK. Thanks, Sergeant. We'll be there in about half an hour. Make sure the scene is preserved, won't you? And don't let anyone leave the place."

"Right, sir. Two of our lads are up there now. I'll tell them to wait till you arrive."

Burke hung up.

"As you've probably guessed, there's been another one. Fiona, Dónal – you're both with me. Séan, will you call Dr O'Higgins and get forensics out too? It's Vico View on the Vico Road in Dalkey. And when you've done that, you'd better let Heffernan know – but wait till we're well out of the way first!"

"Yes, sure, boss. Good luck."

* * *

There was a sombre mood in Burke's car as they drove out towards the normally peaceful coastal village of Dalkey. Moore was in the front passenger's seat, with Lawler in the back and Burke driving. As they sped along the Blackrock bypass, blue lights and sirens helping them to cut through the mid-morning traffic, Burke said, "I think we need to get the shrinks in. We need to find out what makes chummy tick – how his twisted little mind works. What do you think?" glancing briefly at his sergeant.

"Can't do any harm, I suppose. But you know I have very little faith in that lot. Too much mumbo-jumbo for my liking."

"Yeah, but Heffernan will be asking why we haven't engaged them if we don't, and then there's the AC to deal with. Can you make a call and see if we can get someone down to the station this afternoon?"

"Yeah, OK. You're right, I suppose."

An Garda Síochána don't have serving officers who are trained psychological profilers, but they have access to a panel of professional psychologists who work in various other departments of the state. Access to these resources is co-ordinated through the Garda's headquarters in the Phoenix Park, and it was there that Moore turned to set up the arrangements. When she had finished the call, she said to Burke, "Right. We've got a Doctor Mairéad Coogan coming in at four o'clock. They tell me that she is very well qualified for the job, so we'll see."

"Great. You'd better let Séan know so he can meet her if we're not back by then," Burke said.

Burke pulled his car up outside Vico View. A uniformed officer was standing at the door, and blue and white crime scene tape had been stretched around the entrance. As they walked across the car park, Burke said to Lawler, "Dónal, will you get a list of the staff and start interviewing anyone who was on duty last night? And get a full list too – that's everyone that works in the place, suppliers, regular visitors – you know the drill."

"Right, boss. What are you two going to do?"

"We're going to wait for forensics. I don't want to risk contaminating the scene till they have had a good chance to examine it. We'll just get the feel of the place, and maybe talk to the owner."

It didn't take him long to find the proprietor. Mrs Molly Webster was an elderly woman, probably well into her seventies. She had short, curly grey hair, and was a little on the heavy side. She was a bit stooped too, and used a walking stick to aid her mobility. Her wrinkled complexion hinted at years of hardship, or at least discontent, and her thin lips curled down at the edges adding to the grim impression that she exuded. Burke introduced himself.

"Mrs Webster, is it?" he said.

"It is. And who or what might you be?" she said dismissively.

"Detective Inspector Aidan Burke. I'm here to investigate the death of one of your residents, Mrs Webster, and I'd appreciate your full co-operation. This is my colleague, Detective Sergeant Moore," he said gesturing towards his partner.

The woman grunted and turned her back on Burke, hobbling off to a small office room at the back of the hall. Burke and Moore followed.

The office was chaotic. It smelled of old dust and grime, and it looked as if the dirty sash window hadn't been opened for many a long day. A small, old, oak desk festooned with files, books and general detritus was jammed into the corner, and old bookcases packed with volumes of all kinds towered precariously over it. Burke felt as if he had stepped right back into the 1950s.

Mrs Webster side-stepped her way gingerly in behind the desk and sat down with a sigh. Burke, although not invited to do so, took up the only other chair in the room, facing the woman, while Moore stood awkwardly just inside the door. Seeing Moore's discomfort, Burke gestured to her, and she left the room to go in search of Lawler. Burke waited for Webster to speak, but when it became clear that no such thing would happen, he began.

"Mrs Webster, what can you tell me about the woman who passed away here last night?"

"Not much. She's been here for a few months. Her niece brought her in. I think she's Miss Finnucane's sister's girl."

"Did she have any regular visitors at all, or any other relatives?"

Webster said nothing, but started exploring the pile of tattered manila folders piled up on the desk. About a third of the way down the pile, she pulled out a file with Miss Finnucane written in thick black marker on its front. She opened the file with her gnarled arthritic hands, and studied the content. Eventually, she looked up.

"There's not much here. The niece is down as next of kin. I have an address if you need it."

"Yes, please, that would be helpful. Was Miss Finnucane healthy, in your view?"

"More or less. Her old bones were a bit creaky like my own, and of course her mind was gone – totally gaga except for a couple of hours every three days or so when she was perfectly lucid. Odd."

"Did she have a doctor in attendance?"

"Not regularly. Dr Fleming used to drop in on her from time to time to see how she was. I think she lived near him in Glenageary before we got her."

"Is that Dr Fleming from St Catherine's Road?"

"I've no idea where he lives, Inspector. Gaunt-looking fellow. Looks as if he could do with a decent meal, but pleasant enough, for a doctor."

"Was Miss Finnucane on any regular medication?"

Webster fumbled through the thin file again.

"Just aspirin. She probably should have been on something stronger, but those meds are very expensive, and I doubt she could afford it."

"Were her fees up to date?"

"Oh, yes, Inspector. We don't allow the residents to get into arrears. It's just too messy, especially if they die. It can take years to get paid what with probate and stuff. No, I insist on payment monthly in advance with a month in hand. You've no idea how costly this place is to run."

"Tell me about your staff, Mrs Webster. Who would have been on duty last night after, say, nine o'clock?"

"I'd have to check. There are two or three Filipino girls that take it in turns at night. I think they may be sisters. They come from Dún Laoghaire. Thankfully, they're relatively cheap."

"Are they qualified nurses?"

"Well, they say they are, but you can never be sure with these types. Their qualifications are all from overseas, but they are very good with the old people. We've never had any trouble – up to now, that is."

"Who would know who was on duty last night?"

"You can ask Anna. She's our administrator. She'll be round and about somewhere. When will your lot be finished up?" Webster said.

"Later today, I imagine. Our forensic team should be here by now. They'll be going over the place for much of the day."

"I suppose this will close us down. Not very good for business, is it?"

Burke was taken aback by the woman's apparent lack of empathy for one of her charges who had almost certainly met her death at the hands of some nutter. He decided there was little to be gained from continuing to talk to her, so he made his excuses and left to go looking for Anna.

Chapter Fourteen

Burke found Anna in the kitchens which were located in an annexe at the back of the property. She was talking to Dónal Lawler while nursing a cup of coffee. Unlike her employer, the Lithuanian girl seemed to be genuinely upset at the goings on in the home. Lawler made the introductions, and Burke sat down, accepting his colleague's offer of a hot drink.

"Hi, Anna. This is a dreadful business. The poor woman. I'm sorry, but I need to ask you some questions about the place here and Miss Finnucane. Is that OK?"

"Yes, yes, of course. But what happened to her? She was fine yesterday. I know she had early signs of dementia, but other than that she was very healthy. I've never seen this before," she said, and sobbed a little into a crumpled tissue.

"I don't know if you are aware, Anna, but there have been some other old ladies that have met a similar fate recently in this area. We think Miss Finnucane may have been killed by the same person."

"Oh, good God. Are you sure?"

"No. Not yet in any case. That's why we need to find out as much as possible about this place. Have you worked here long?"

"I've been here for three years now. I have a degree in business administration from home, so I got this job when I came here."

"How do you enjoy working here?"

"It's OK. Mrs Webster is a little – how do you say – tight. The pay isn't much, but I enjoy the old people. They are very nice, and good fun too most of the time. They are so funny."

"Tell me about Miss Finnucane. Did she have any regular visitors?" Burke said.

"Your friend was asking me. Her niece came to see her sometimes in the evenings. But Maeve wasn't good after tea, not usually anyway. So, she never stayed long."

"When was she last here?"

"Hmmm... about a week ago, I think. I can check the visitors' book if you like."

"Yes, please, Anna. But there's no hurry. Was there anyone else?"

"Wait. Yes. A couple of days ago, her nephew, Jeremy, came to see her. I remember, because she wasn't having a good day, and he brought some of her favourite chocolates. In fact, she gave them to the nurse. She said she didn't like them. I thought it was strange."

"Had Jeremy been before?"

"No, never. Not when I have been here anyway."

"Did Miss Finnucane recognise this Jeremy?" Burke said.

"No, not at all, but that doesn't surprise me. You have to realise she was getting quite bad."

"Was there anything else odd about Jeremy, Anna?"

"Just that he went upstairs to leave the chocolates in Maeve's room. He said he wanted to see where she slept. I thought it was a bit funny, but he seemed nice."

"Did you go up with him?"

"No. I have to stay at the desk unless I'm on a break. Mrs Webster is very particular about that."

"Would you be able to describe this man for us, Anna? I mean properly. Maybe work with a police artist to make a picture of him?"

"Maybe. He was only here for a few minutes, but I could try."

"Thanks. That would be most helpful. Dónal, Sergeant Lawler here will arrange it."

* * *

By the time Burke had finished with Anna, the forensic team had arrived and were crawling all over the upstairs landing, and what had been Maeve Finnucane's bedroom. As Burke climbed the stairs, he could see a shape in a white scene-of-crime suit down on its knees examining the floor outside room 12. Burke approached carefully, stepping on the yellow pads that had been placed on the floor so as not to contaminate the scene.

"Anything?" he said to the bent over shape.

A girl with pretty blue eyes looked up at him from behind her mask. "Maybe," she said, pulling down the fabric covering from her face. "There seem to be some footprints here that were made by a wet shoe. They come and go from the end where the fire escape is. I'll know more in a little while, Inspector."

"Anything else you can tell me?" Burke said.

The girl looked back up at the senior officer with a slightly withering look, as if to say 'let me get on with it' but instead she simply replied, "There's nothing odd about the print. Standard Clarks fare from what I can see. But there may be an uneven wear pattern on the left shoe. I can't be sure yet. I need more time."

"Point taken, eh…"

"Marian, Sir. Sergeant Marian Byrne. Excuse me if I don't shake hands," she said, returning to her painstaking work.

Inside number 12 two more suited officers were busy examining the room in fine detail, and Fiona Moore had donned vinyl gloves and was having a good look around on the dressing table and in the drawers.

"What have we got, Phil?" Burke said, addressing a man that he recognised, largely by his stature – he was nearly six foot six inches tall.

"Hello, Aidan. Very little actually. A couple of footprints that match the ones that are out on the corridor. I think this pillow was used to suffocate her," the man said pointing to an item propped against the wall under the window, "I'll be checking the fibres later – there are some fragments in her mouth and nostrils."

"Has Dr O'Higgins been?" Burke asked.

"Yes. He confirmed time of death at sometime between ten and midnight last night. He says it could be the same M. O. as the others – an injection, followed up with smothering. He said to tell you he'll be doing the PM at three o'clock, and he'll confirm it then."

"Yes, we'll be along. Have you found anything of interest, Sergeant?" he said, turning to Moore.

"No, nothing. Just a couple of very old magazines, oh, and her purse. There's thirty-five euro in it and a few other bits and pieces. I'll bag it up."

The young attractive girl in the white suit came back into the room.

"You might like to see this, Inspector," she said, gesturing towards the corridor.

Burke and Moore both followed her along the passage making sure to use the steps provided, so as not to contaminate the floor. When they reached the fire escape, the white-suited girl bent down and pointed with her pen at the edge of the fire door.

"There are some recent scratches here. Look – just here near the locking mechanism. And it looks as if something has been taped onto the door and the door jamb too. There's no sign of any bits of the stuff left behind, but I might be able to get an analysis from the sticky residue to see what type of thing it was."

"Hmm. Do you think that's how he got in, assuming it was a man?" Moore said.

"Yes. Looks like it. The footprints started off quite wet and they dry out as they move towards the door of room 12. The guys working outside have got some pretty good impressions from the base of the fire escape too. There's soft clay down there on top of the tarmac," the girl said.

"OK. Thanks. Well keep at it. See if you can get anything else, no matter how insignificant it might appear. Catch you later," Burke said.

The forensic girl didn't appreciate being told how to do her job, but she stayed quiet and just got on with it. Sometimes, she thought, these hot-shot detectives really had ideas about themselves.

Chapter Fifteen

"I'm going across to see what the PM reveals. Can you talk to the profiler woman at four o'clock? I should be back before you've finished," Burke said to Moore when they arrived back into the station in Store Street. They had stopped at Finnegan's in Dalkey for an early lunch after they had finished up at Vico View, and had enjoyed the much-celebrated fish pie that the gastro-pub was famous for, followed by a delicious fruit and berry crumble garnished with both cream and ice cream – also a speciality. Burke resisted the temptation to have an alcoholic drink, though he was sorely tempted.

"Yes, fine. I'm not sure she will be much use to us, but we'd better go through the motions in any case, if only to keep Heffernan off our backs," Moore said.

"I agree. I imagine it will be good old detective work that will catch this bugger. He'll be getting cocky now, having got away with three killings, and that's when they start to make mistakes. By the way, how many care homes are there in the south Dublin area – say from Stillorgan to Shankill?" Burke said.

"I haven't a clue – but I can find out. Why?"

"We may have to be seen to be doing something with all of them. I doubt if we have the resources to post a watch on them all individually, but the public will expect something. Find out how many there are and think about what we might do, will you?"

"Yes, OK. But there's nothing to say he will stick to the Southside. I mean, if he sees that we have put some security measures in place, all he has to do is move across the river and carry on. We can't cover them all."

"I know that," Burke said, somewhat impatiently, "it's just optics, Sergeant, optics. We have to be seen to be taking some positive action. Look, I'd better get going. See you a bit later."

Burke didn't like post-mortems, so on the way over to the mortuary, he ducked into the pub opposite the station and downed a large whiskey very quickly.

"Thanks, Danny. I'll see you later."

He left a ten euro note on the bar.

* * *

Dr Mairéad Coogan arrived at Store Street a few minutes before four o'clock and asked for Sergeant Moore at the front desk. The woman was in her forties, tall and slim, and wore a grey, business-like trouser suit with a pale pink blouse beneath. She was not unattractive, with an open, oval face surrounded by a mop of dark blonde hair, casually styled, down to her shoulders. Her makeup, if she was using any at all, was very understated, and as a result, she had a very natural appearance.

Moore introduced herself, and they shook hands awkwardly as Dr Coogan transferred the black leather portfolio she was carrying to her left hand to execute the greeting. As they made their way upstairs to Burke's office, the two women exchanged the usual meaningless chat that goes between new acquaintances as they attempt to get their bearings with each other.

"Where are you based?" Moore said.

"I work all over. My consulting rooms are on Fitzwilliam Square, but I find myself doing more and more work for the Gardaí these days, so I'm up at the Park a lot."

"Lovely," Moore said sarcastically, "I find that place very austere. Gives me the creeps."

"I know what you mean, but it doesn't bother me. The work is always interesting. That's what counts."

Moore sat in behind Burke's desk, and Mairéad Coogan took the seat in front of her and unzipped her briefcase, taking out a yellow jotter pad and an expensive Mont Blanc pen.

"So, what have you got that you need me for?" she said.

Moore went on to explain the full circumstances of the three deaths at the old peoples' homes, including as much detail as she could recall. Coogan stayed silent while Moore was speaking, but made several notes on her pad, which Moore observed were in a very neat hand and well organised on the page. Moore finished her story by asking the doctor what her initial thoughts were.

"It's not much to go on, Sergeant. Not yet anyway. Have you managed to establish any connection at all between the three old ladies, or even the homes they were living in?"

"No, we haven't. There's one common denominator between two of the homes – the GP that attended the first victim also attends some of the patients in the last place. But that's about it. We've checked him out, and I can't see that he's involved."

"Hmm. Anything else common to the victims?"

"Like what?" Moore said.

"Age? Previous professions? Place of birth? Marital status or any connections via their deceased husbands – that sort of thing."

"We haven't done that much detailed analysis. Should we?"

"As I see it, there are three possibilities. One – the killings are entirely random. The killer just picks them because it's easy to get into the homes, and for some reason he's not suspected. Two – he's on a mission to rid the world of a particular type of old lady. Something in their past or present connects them. Or three – he was only actually after one specific victim, and the other two were just a cover. That's the least likely scenario in my view, but shouldn't be ruled out altogether."

"Will he kill again?" Moore said.

"Yes, very probably. He may have already achieved his goal, whatever that was, but once he gets the taste for it – and so far, it's been very easy for him – he probably won't be able to help himself. I think you can expect more of the same, Sergeant. Sorry."

"Terrific! How the hell do we get ahead of him then?"

"Data. That's the key. Somewhere in all that you've told me – and the bits you left out because you didn't think they were important – lies the key to all this. Do you have AccuDet?"

"I don't think so. What is it?" Moore said.

"It's amazing. You feed in all the information that you have about a crime – or a series of crimes – and it produces a prediction of where and when such crimes are likely to reoccur. Like everything else with computer software, the better the information that goes in, the better the result. But you have a lot of data points. That will help. Have you got a decent computer person on the team?"

"We have Séan – he's pretty good."

"OK. Well, get him access to the software – the Gardaí have a license – and then get every single piece of information you can scavenge and ask him to put it in. Then get him to do around 1,000 runs with it, and see what it suggests."

"OK. We can do that. But what about the perpetrator himself? What can you tell us about him?"

"He's a loner. Almost certainly lives on his own, probably in a slightly grotty flat somewhere. He's probably unemployed, or just possibly a shift worker, but more likely unemployed. He's no older than 50, possibly a good bit younger. Confident. Friendly disposition. Maybe even a bit of a charmer. The kind of bloke you could easily have a chat with when you are out for a walk, or in the pub."

"What about motive?" Moore said.

"That's very tricky. My guess is that there's some kind of complex going on there – like maybe he was rejected or ridiculed by his mother, or even his grandmother at an early age. In his own twisted logic, he's getting even. But that's just speculation on my part. And it's not much help anyway. What about the drugs he's using?"

"Standard clinical grade morphine. We found an empty 15cc phial under the bed of the first victim, but it didn't tell us much. It's the kind you could get at any pharmacy or hospital dispensary," Moore replied.

"Yes, but you can't just walk into a chemist's shop and buy three or more phials of morphine over the counter, unless you have a medical connection of some kind. Even then, it has to be registered and you'd have to give your details. I know it's a drudge, but I think you should check with all the pharmacies in the Blackrock, Dún Laoghaire, Glenageary, Dalkey area to see if anyone has been buying the stuff in bulk. And it might be worth checking with the doctors in the area too," Coogan said.

"Crikey! That will take a small army. I'll have to talk to the boss about getting more resources on board. Anything else you can think of?" Moore asked.

"Not at the moment. I'd like to talk to Séan when he gets AccuDet up and running. Go over the output with him and see if it tells us anything. If you like I can hang around for a while and give him a hand to set it up."

"Could you? That would be great, thanks."

Part Two

Chapter Sixteen

The man awoke at his usual time of seven-thirty and climbed out of his scruffy bed. He had a quick wash and a shave, and put on his work clothes. He wouldn't bother with breakfast – he'd have a cuppa and maybe a breakfast roll when he got to work.

It was just on eight o'clock when he pulled the old Nissan round the back of the school and parked. He got out, not bothering to lock the car, and went across to the wooden door that gave access to his workshop underneath the main school building. He opened the door and went in. He took the kettle from the bench and filled it from the tap that was just outside the building, and lit the small gas ring, putting the water on to boil for tea.

He sat down in the very tatty armchair that he had rescued from the skip last year, and opened the paper that he had bought when he was getting his breakfast roll in the Spar shop on the way to St Cyprian's School in between Ranelagh and Rathmines, about two miles from his home. The school had originally been a monastery, but when the state was established in 1922, it had been taken over and given to the Catholic Church to run as a national or primary school. Initially it accommodated just sixty boys between the ages of four and eleven, but during the 1950s, with the huge growth in suburban housing in the area, new buildings had been added, and further additions were made in the 1960s and 1970s, so that now there was a hotchpotch of different architectures that housed nearly three hundred pupils, both boys and girls.

The headmaster was a lean and angular individual with a sombre disposition and allegedly lacking any vestige of a sense of humour. But the man had found him OK to deal with, even if he was a bit brusque. It was he who appeared in the doorway of the workshop just as the kettle began to boil.

"Ah, Damian, you're in," the headmaster said rather unnecessarily, "I have a few little jobs for you today. Firstly, there's one of the wash basins in the staff room toilet that's leaking again. Mrs Ketterick is whinging about it as usual. See if you can sort it out, will you?"

"Yes, of course, headmaster. By rights, it needs a whole new sink and fittings. But I'll see if I can patch it up for the moment. Is there something else?"

"Yes, there is. The lock on my office door is acting up again. It took me nearly five minutes to close it last night when I was leaving, and today I thought I might be locked out altogether. You'd better fit a new one. I can't be messing with that sort of thing."

"Right, sir. I'll go down to the hardware shop in Ranelagh and get a new one as soon as they're open and see to it. Do you have the key?"

"The key?" the headmaster said.

"Yes. I'll need the key to open the door and remove the lock so I can show it to the man in the shop as a pattern."

"Oh, right. Yes, of course. I'll leave it with the secretary. She'll be in shortly."

With that, the headmaster turned on his heels and left without as much as a thank you or goodbye. But Damian was used to his manner and it didn't bother him. Damian worked as handyman and general dog's body at the school four mornings each week during term time and two mornings during the holidays. There was never enough time to do the long list of jobs that the school secretary kept adding to each day, and as a result, the teaching staff thought Damian to be quite lazy and rather useless. But he was all the school could afford, and it suited him well enough, giving him lots of free time in the afternoons and on Fridays, when he didn't work at all.

The headmaster and the school secretary were housed in what had been the original building of the monastery dating back to the early nineteenth century. The building was well proportioned, with high ceilings and wide, tiled corridors, and suffered just a small amount of dilapidation caused by a leaky gutter that led to some dampness and black mould high up on the whitewashed walls.

Damian approached the woman and asked for the key to the headmaster's office.

"Oh, yes. He told me you'd be looking for it. I put it away safely. Here it is. Will you be long working on it?" the woman said. The woman was in her fifties and rather frumpish, but easy enough to get along with, Damian thought, even if she was sometimes impatient with him when her list of necessary repairs got a little out of hand.

"I'll be as long as it takes, Mrs Ketterick. But I'll have it all fixed up by lunchtime, don't worry."

Mrs Ketterick said nothing, and handed over the key.

Damian had no trouble removing the damaged lock from the polished dark oak door that guarded the office of the headmaster. As it was a nice morning, he decided to walk down to the hardware shop, where the man who ran the place singlehandedly knew him well. He soon procured a replacement of the same type and size and was back fixing it in the door before the school paused for the mid-morning break. He turned the key four or five times in the lock to ensure that it was doing its job properly, and then handed the three shiny brass keys to Mrs Ketterick. Before she could regale him with her famous 'list', Damian was off.

Back in his workshop, he equipped himself with some plumbing tools, a few bits and pieces of white plastic pipework and a roll of strong waterproof tape. He then went back into the main building and into the staff room. This room was one of the nicest in the whole school. It had originally looked out over well-tended lawns, but these days the view was impaired by the presence of yet another block of hastily built and architecturally uninspiring concrete classrooms. It was a square room of generous dimensions, and opening off it was a bathroom that comprised two cubicles and two hand basins. There had been many requests to provide separate male and female facilities for the staff to use, but these had been put on the long finger for budgetary reasons, so the teachers – more or less evenly divided between the genders – had to make do with a 'unisex' arrangement.

Inside the facility, the old Victorian basins were cracked and crazed, but Damian set about yet another makeshift repair to see if he could stop the water leaking out onto the shoes of whoever was washing their hands at the time. As he got to work, he recalled his own school days with mounting anger and resentment.

Damian was one of five children born to a stevedore and his wife. In those days, container traffic hadn't completely taken over, so there was good work to be had in Dublin's docks, loading and unloading loose cargo such as timber, coal, grain and other mixed commodities. Damian lived with his father, mother and four siblings in a tenement building on Fenian Street, and attended the local national school situated at the junction of the River Liffey and Moss Street. Damian was one of fifty-eight pupils, and the entire school was run by an unpleasant old woman who lacked any evidence of empathy towards her charges.

On many an occasion, Damian would put his hand up seeking permission to go to the rudimentary toilet facilities which occupied a draughty shed in the back yard of the school.

"Yes, what is it, Damian?" the teacher would enquire impatiently.

"Please miss, I need to go to the toilet," the six-year-old would reply.

"Nonsense. You're just trying to avoid doing your sums. Stay where you are!"

Minutes later, he ventured to repeat his request, but to no avail. Eventually, with no other choice, Damian would wet his pants, as he couldn't hold on any longer. The teacher, her ears constantly tuned for any unusual sound in the classroom, would hear the steady flow of urine onto the school's wooden floor, and would march to Damian's desk, grab him by the collar and haul him up to the front of the room where he would be ridiculed in front of his peers, much to their delight.

"Get outside, you dirty boy. You can stay in the yard and listen through the window. And what's more, you can stay behind at two o'clock and clean your mess up. You disgust me!" she would shriek, thrusting the young miscreant out through the school door.

This happened several times during Damian's primary education. Nor was he alone in his humiliation. Several other boys suffered the same fate, although the girls seemed to fare better – perhaps they had a greater bladder capacity.

Why was this not reported, you may wonder. In those days, it was absolutely unheard of for children to say anything negative about anyone in authority. It's how some priests got away with the most heinous acts of paedophilia for so long in Ireland. Any attempt to bring such mistreatment to the attention of parents would be met with a severe beating and total disbelief. And so, Damian's early years were punctuated by this cruelty which sewed in his mind a vicious hatred of female teachers that grew and festered as he got older.

When he had finished the two urgent tasks, Damian took another three jobs off the secretary's list and attended to them. There was a broken chair in one of the classrooms where a rather corpulent pupil had leaned back on it, and the legs had simply folded up beneath him. A light switch in another room was fizzing and sparking. This was not an unusual occurrence. The electrics in the older part of the school were in poor condition. Finally, as the clock wound its way around to lunchtime, Damian eased out a sticking cupboard door in the kitchens, and then he was done for the day.

When he got home, he took a carton of soup from the fridge and set it to heat on the stove. He was in a reflective mood. On the one hand he felt satisfied that he had achieved his primary objective. He had avenged all the cruelty that the horrid bitch had meted out to him, and many others over the years. But he still felt, at least to some extent, unsettled. He had enjoyed the excitement and adventure that had punctuated his otherwise dull life. The preparation, the possibility of being caught, sneaking around late at night in the homes, the actual act of injecting the women and then smothering them till they stopped breathing had all stimulated parts of him that he didn't even know existed. And he had to admit that he had enjoyed it. As his soup began to bubble in the pot, he said to himself, "Maybe just one more, then I'll stop."

Chapter Seventeen

Moore was still sitting at Aidan Burke's desk when the phone rang.

"Hello. Is that the officer who is investigating the sudden death of Miss Finnucane?" a woman's voice on the other end of the call said.

"Yes, that's right. I'm Detective Sergeant Moore, and I'm assigned to that case. May I ask who's calling please?"

"Oh, yes, sorry. My name is Marcella Kane from Kane and Clotworthy. We're estate agents in Sandycove. I'm handling the sale of Miss Finnucane's bungalow, but I've been told she has died in suspicious circumstances. Is that right?"

"Yes, I'm afraid so, but I can't go into details just now, Miss Kane."

"No, I understand. That's fine. But it's just there's something that may be of interest, that's all."

"Oh? Do go on."

Marcella Kane went on to describe what she had been told about the man who had been snooping around a few days before the woman died.

"You see, the thing is – well it could be nothing really – but he never called the office. And Mr Harris – that's the man who lives next door to Miss Finnucane's house – said he appeared to be interested in buying the place as a fixer-upper. It's probably not important, but I thought it was a bit odd."

"I see. Yes, I agree, it does sound a bit strange OK. What did you say the neighbour's name was?" Moore said.

"Harris. Mr Harris, and he lives right next door to where Miss Finnucane lived up to the time she moved into the nursing home."

Moore took down the address for Harris, and thanked Marcella Kane for calling.

"I suppose we'll have to take it off the market now," Kane said, "it's a shame, because I have a young couple who are very keen."

"Well, I think you should talk to Miss Finnucane's solicitor about that, Miss Kane. It's nothing to do with us really."

"Oh, sorry, yes I know. Oh well. I hope you get to the bottom of it all soon anyway." With that she was gone.

Moore went and collected Dónal Lawler from the open plan office.

"C'mon, Dónal. We're going for a drive out to sunny Sandycove by the sea."

On the way out in the car, Moore explained what she had been told by the estate agent.

"Doesn't sound too promising, boss. He could have been anyone. Just because he didn't follow up with her doesn't mean there was anything sinister about it," Lawler said.

"You're right, Dónal. But it's a coincidence. And you know what Burke says about those!" Moore said.

"Fair enough. Best to check it out, I guess. Sure, what else would we be doing on a fine afternoon in any case?"

Moore gave her colleague a wilting look.

* * *

Moore pulled the car up outside the dilapidated bungalow with the Kane and Clotworthy 'For Sale' board in the front garden, and they both got out. There was a man in the front garden of the next bungalow along. He was tending to the immaculate lawn, bent down, prising a stray dandelion up out of the soil carefully, so as not to disturb the carpet-like surface more than absolutely necessary.

Moore approached him and said with a smile, "In other times, you'd be keeping that and making coffee substitute from the root!"

"Oh, hello. Yes, I suppose you are right. Damn things. The seeds blow in from Miss Finnucane's. I do wish they'd get it sold to someone who would take a bit of pride in the place," he said, looking disparagingly at the broken-down dwelling.

"Mr Harris, I presume?" Moore said.

The man took on a puzzled expression.

"Yes, that's right. Who are you?"

Moore introduced them both, and the man invited them into his beloved garden.

"How can I help, officer?" he said when they had all sat down on the green wrought iron chairs surrounding a small white table near the door to his house.

Moore explained the call she had taken from Marcella Kane earlier on.

"Do you remember this man at all, Mr Harris?"

"Yes, I do as it happens. I'm nearly always out here in the garden tipping away at something or other. I remember him, because he seemed to arrive on foot quite out of the blue. And he was curious about what had become of the owner of Miss Finnucane's house. He wanted to know if she was dead, of all things!"

"And what did you tell him?" Lawler asked.

"I told him that she was very much alive, but had moved into Vico View over in Dalkey as she had become rather poorly. Did I do the wrong thing?" Harris said.

"Did he ask anything much about the property?" Moore said.

"What sort of thing?"

"Well, like how many bedrooms it has – I presume all these bungalows have more or less the same accommodation."

"No, he didn't, now that you mention it. He seemed more interested in the owner than the house. But I think he took a note of the agent's number from the board in the garden – at least I think he may have done. Oh dear, I'm not much good at this, am I?"

"It's fine, Mr Harris, don't worry. I wonder if you could give us a description of the man?"

Harris went on to describe the man's height and stature, and his hairstyle, or lack of one, before admitting, "I'm really sorry, officer, but he was only here for a few minutes. I should have taken more notice. Do you think he is connected to what happened at all?"

"It's very hard to tell, but we need to check every possibility out carefully, nonetheless. Don't worry, you've been very helpful. Here's my card in case anything else comes to mind. Give me a call anytime." Moore and Lawler got up, thanked the man again, and left.

* * *

On the way back to town, Lawler asked Moore what she thought.

"We need to check Harris's description with the girl at Vico View – what was her name?"

"Eh, Anna, I think – yes, that's it, Anna," Lawler said.

"Have we got the description she gave of Miss Finnucane's mysterious visitor back at the station?"

"Yes. I think she did a sketch too."

"Great. If these two are even close, then we may be on to something."

Chapter Eighteen

Braemore House, situated at the foot of Corbawn Lane in Shankill, had once been the residence of a well-heeled accountant and his family. But during the 1980s recession, the man had fallen on hard times, and he had sold out to a Mr and Mrs McKinley who intended to operate the house as a retirement home.

The McKinleys were Irish by birth, but had spent many years in the USA where they had accumulated considerable wealth. On their return to Ireland, they sought out and purchased Braemore House for its accommodation, and its unique position right on the edge of the coast with magnificent views out over the Irish Sea, not to mention its peaceful location at the end of a *cul-de-sac*. The house was on a large plot of nearly two acres, and had much of that space to the rear, making an extension to the building entirely feasible, subject of course to the necessary permissions.

Soon after the McKinleys acquired the place, they set about adding to it, providing twenty-four additional bedrooms over two floors, and a large dining room, a recreation room, a library and a small gymnasium. They had also had a lift installed against the cliff that went from the foot of the front garden down to the beach some 30 feet below, to facilitate less able-bodied residents, or those in wheelchairs. Steps were provided for those who were more agile.

Andrew McKinley was an astute businessman. When the property had been fully prepared, and passed all the necessary safety regulations, drawing much praise from the team of inspectors who assured him that he had exceeded requirements by some measure, he set about attracting customers.

The target group were well-to-do retirees drawn from an academic background, who would have no issue raising the not insubstantial fees that the McKinleys intended to charge for their hospitality. McKinley argued that it was advantageous for all concerned that the residents should be of roughly equal intellectual ability, so that they could converse and debate amongst themselves as they grew older. To encourage such activity a well-stocked library was installed, and three dedicated PCs connected to the internet were made available for research on any topic that was causing puzzlement or argument.

McKinley advertised the facility in such academic journals as stooped low enough to carry paid advertisements, and other publications read by his potential customers. He also circulated information about the home to the universities and private members clubs where academics were likely to be members. Before long, the home had filled up with 24 residents all drawn from the target demographic. Of course, they were from mixed disciplines. Some were merely retired secondary teachers, but there was a good mixture of lecturers, researchers, professors and one or two that had achieved some notoriety for their published works on specialist topics. Mercifully, more by design than by accident, they were all in quite good health and had opted for residential care more for convenience than out of need for intense medical attention.

Damian, still feeling somewhat unfulfilled, spotted the advertisement on a page from a discarded publication that he had rescued from the rubbish left out from the staff room at the school where he worked. He found it amusing to read through these old magazines during his tea break or at lunchtime, and the ad for Braemore House caught his attention. He liked the 'intellectually stimulating environment' that the advert promised, and the reference to 'suitable for retired academics, with a comprehensive library and research facilities'.

Damian tore the small scrap of paper from the magazine and folded it carefully, putting it away in the pocket of his overalls. On Friday, he would call the home, and, pretending to be the son of an elderly maths teacher, he would arrange to visit Braemore House to see the lay of the land.

* * *

Burke called the team together for a briefing late in the afternoon. He started by telling them that Heffernan and those above him were hopping mad. It wasn't helped by the headline in the Evening Herald that read, 'Lock up your Grandparents!'. The front-page article went on to describe how the population of all the retirement homes in Ireland were now living in fear of their lives from the mysterious murderer, and that he could strike again at any time, apparently with impunity.

Burke threw the paper down on a nearby desk.

"Right. So, what have we, Dónal?"

"Well, sir, Mr Harris, the man who lived next door to Maeve Finnucane, and the receptionist from Vico View have both given a similar description for our person of interest. We've worked up an e-fit," Lawler said, producing several sheets of A4 paper with what looked like a pencil drawing of a man on them.

"OK. Well get that circulated to all and sundry, including the media. Let's see if we can get them doing something for us instead of throwing stones. Send it out to all the care homes in the Dublin area too and ask them to be on the lookout for this man, and to report any sightings immediately. Anything else?"

Séan O'Reilly raised his hand tentatively.

"Yes, Séan, what is it?" Burke said.

"I've been doing some work with AccuDet, sir. I spent the afternoon inputting all the information we have so far, and I did 1,000 runs of the software just as Mairéad – I mean Dr Coogan – showed me."

Burke interrupted, "Séan, I'm sure that's fascinating, but I don't think a computer is going to solve this one for us."

Moore was unhappy at the way O'Reilly had been put down, so she spoke out.

"Hold on, sir. Let's hear what he has to say at least."

Burke looked at O'Reilly scornfully.

"Well?" he said.

"Thanks, sir. It came out with something which may or may not be connected. About five months ago, a Doctor Willoughby's surgery in Rathgar was broken into at night. Quite a bit of stuff was taken, including five 15cc phials of morphine. The software made the link on account of the way in which the old ladies had been injected. It may be nothing. Do you think it's worth following up, sir?" O'Reilly said.

"Hmm... could be. Why don't you get onto Willoughby and get a list of all his patients and put them into your computer thingy. Oh, and does it take pictures?" Burke said.

"Eh, I'm not sure, sir, but I'll find out."

"On second thoughts, Fiona, maybe you should pay the good doctor a visit and bring a picture of chummy here with you – see if it rings any bells. You might catch him at home this evening if you're lucky. Did forensics identify the empty morphine bottle we found at Cedar Hill as being from the same stock as they keep there in the medicine cupboard?" Burke said.

"I'm not sure, sir. I'll have to check that in their report. I'll get on it as soon as we're finished here," Moore said.

"OK. Now what about security at the old folks' homes. What have we done about that?"

"I've been onto all the stations on the southside and asked them to increase patrols between nine-thirty and midnight around the homes. And we've circulated all of the properties too, advising them to increase security. That didn't go down too well though. Most of them seem strapped for cash, though I'm not sure I believe them. If we could even get them to lock their bloody doors that would be something, but they keep bleating on about their premises not being a prison, and they don't want their residents to feel incarcerated. I reminded one or two of the snottier ones that they don't want their residents to feel dead either!"

"Excellent PR as usual, Fiona – not! Let's hope Heffernan doesn't get to hear of it, or worse still the AC! Anything from forensics?"

"They recovered some small soil samples from the shoe prints at Vico View. It was mostly from the grounds it seems, but there were some other small bits of soil mixed up with it too. They're doing an analysis now to see if they can get a geo match," Moore said.

"What's that?" Burke asked.

"They have a database of all the different soil types from all over the country, and if they can match the fragments that they recovered from the shoe prints, they may be able to tell roughly where it came from, or maybe even better than that," Moore said.

"More computerized wizardry! At this rate, you and me will soon be redundant, Sergeant."

Before leaving the station to drive out to Rathgar, Moore checked the forensic report on the first death at Cedar Hill. She discovered that the empty phial of morphine discovered beneath Fidelma Humphries' bed, was not in fact from the same source as the drug stored rather casually in the nursing homes' medicine cabinet.

"Now, how the hell did we miss that!" she exclaimed.

Chapter Nineteen

Dr Arthur Willoughby occupied a fine red-bricked residence about halfway up the Rathgar Road. It was semi-detached, but that took nothing from its grandeur, with twelve granite steps up to the glossy front door, adorned with polished brass fittings, and surmounted by a semi-circular stained-glass fanlight.

The garden level accommodation had been allocated to the doctor's surgery, and was identified by a tasteful and discreet sign directing patients to the door. The entrance was concealed from view from the road, as it was placed in the side of the steps up to the main house.

In front of the house, the garden had been divided between parking space for the doctor's car and one or two patients' vehicles, and a very tidy arrangement of a small lawn with a flower bed border. There was no sign of the unsightly green, brown and black plastic wheelie-bins that one is obliged to use these days, leading Moore to surmise that there must be a back entrance to the property, probably opening onto a lane at the rear.

Moore went initially to the surgery door, where the attendance times were helpfully displayed. Noting that today's surgery had concluded over an hour ago, she decided to climb the steps and call to the residential part of the property, hoping that the doctor was at home.

Moore rang the ceramic bell-push and waited. After what seemed like several minutes, but may have been less, the door opened wide and a tall, thin, grey-haired man dressed in an immaculate navy pinstripe suit, a bright white shirt, silk tie and highly polished black leather shoes greeted her.

"Yes, how can I help?" the man enquired politely.

"Dr Willoughby?" Moore said, offering her warrant card to the man who took it and studied it momentarily. Moore felt certain that the doctor probably needed reading glasses to see the small print on the card, but he was at least able to identify Moore's profession. When Moore sensed that he had absorbed enough information, she said, "I wonder if I could have a word, Doctor?"

"Yes, of course, Sergeant, please, come in," he said standing back and waving her into the house. The hallway was tiled in small Victorian tiles of beige, ruby red and dark blue that formed a geometrical pattern. There was wainscoting halfway up the walls in what looked like rich mahogany, and above the dado rail, plain, pale green walls were adorned with several large gilt-framed pictures, some of which, at first glance at least, looked valuable. To the right, a stair with a rich deep red carpet and polished mahogany bannister rail ascended gently to the upper floor of the house.

The doctor ushered Moore into the room on the left of the hallway. The room, of Palladian proportions with a magnificent bay window looking out to the front, complete with an upholstered window seat, housed two large sofas facing each other either side of the carved marble fireplace. Various other items of shiny mahogany furniture gave the room a comfy atmosphere, all helped by the magnificent cut-velvet drapes and rich, luxurious carpet.

Willoughby gestured for Moore to take a seat on one of the sofas, and he sat opposite, positioning himself well back and crossing his legs in a relaxed manner. Moore waited a moment for the doctor to speak, but sensing that he was a man who was economical with words, she broke the silence herself.

"Doctor, I believe you had a break in here some time ago, and that some phials of morphine were stolen, amongst other things. Is that right?"

"Oh, yes. That was a few months back. It's an occupational hazard in my line of work, Sergeant. But I've increased security substantially on the surgery now. I've even put iron bars on all the windows, and CCTV all over the place. I don't think it will happen again. Why do you ask now, Sergeant? Frankly the Gardaí didn't take too much interest at the time it happened."

"You may have seen in the papers that some old people have been killed in residential homes recently. Without giving too much away, Doctor, morphine was involved."

"I see. Yes, I did read about that. But why do you think there may be a connection to the break-in here?"

"We have no specific evidence that that is the case, but it's at least a coincidence, and my boss doesn't like coincidences. May I ask who your supplier is? Would the morphine have been branded in any way?"

"I'd have to check that up – my secretary does all the ordering. But, yes, I think the containers do have some sort of proprietary label. Why don't we go downstairs and have a look?"

Moore followed the doctor back out into the hallway, and down three steps towards the rear of the house where a door just outside the expansive kitchen-diner, set in under the main staircase, led to steep stone steps descending to the garden level surgery.

"Be careful here, Sergeant. It's quite steep."

The steps finished in another door which Dr Willoughby opened with a key, and immediately the sound of an alarm alert came on, indicating that he had a minute or so to enter the correct code in order to avoid the thing going off. He stepped up to a concealed keypad and entered the appropriate number, whereupon the system helpfully advised him that the alarm had been turned off.

They had arrived in a waiting room, which was surprisingly spacious and comfortable. There were three further doors off the room. One was clearly the entrance that opened into a small vestibule giving access to the door from outside that Moore had seen earlier, while the other two were identified by neat signs fitted to the centre panel of each, reading 'Office' and 'Surgery' respectively.

Willoughby opened the door to the surgery, and invited Moore in. There was the usual arrangement of furniture one would expect in such a facility, and Moore noted the presence of the CCTV camera the doctor had told her about earlier, attached to the ceiling and partially disguised as a smoke alarm.

In front of the doctor's desk, up against the wall, was a tall white metal cabinet with two narrow doors. The cabinet was secured by a serious-looking combination lock. Dr Willoughby went to it, input a series of six numbers and the lock clicked, allowing him to open the cupboard which was very full of medications of various kinds and other rather grim looking paraphernalia.

"I change the combination every month, Sergeant, and I'm the only one who knows what it is. And as you can see, the window has iron bars on it, and there's a camera in the ceiling as well. Sometimes I feel like I'm in Fort Knox!"

"Yes, very thorough, Doctor. Do you keep much morphine here?"

"Let's see."

The doctor went to a small white box on the highest shelf in the medicine chest, and took it down.

"Just two doses here at the moment. We use it very little, Sergeant, only in emergencies really, like when someone comes in with a serious injury, or is in extreme pain."

"May I see?" Moore asked.

The doctor showed her the small glass phials of the deadly liquid neatly lined up like toy soldiers in what had been a box of six.

"Would you mind if I took a photograph of these?"

"No, not at all. Feel free."

As Moore took out her mobile phone to capture an image of the drug, she said, "Would these be from the same supplier as the ones that were stolen?"

"I imagine so. We've used the same wholesaler for all our medications for years. I'm sure they are."

"Thanks, Doctor, that's fine. By the way, I hope you don't mind me asking, but what is your typical patient like? I mean age, background, that sort of thing."

"They are mostly of the older generation, generally well-heeled, mostly retired professionals. Young people don't seem to need a doctor much. But I have a few *pro bono* patients as well who are troubled – usually by addiction of some kind, or some other issues. They are a lot younger."

"OK, thanks very much for your help. There's just one more thing," she said, taking out the e-fit sketch of their suspect and unfolding it for Willoughby. This time, the doctor did don reading glasses, and took the page from Moore.

"Do you by any chance recognise this man, Doctor?"

Willoughby studied the drawing for a few moments, tilting his head slightly as if to improve his concentration.

"It's not very good, is it?"

"No, I'm afraid not, but it's all we've got."

The doctor handed the page back to Moore, and removed his glasses, putting the right-hand arm of the spectacles into his mouth pensively.

"I really can't be sure, Sergeant, but there may be some similarity to a fellow who used to do a bit of gardening for me. I haven't seen him in months – he was always unreliable. But he used to come on Fridays sometimes and cut the grass, weed the flower beds, that sort of thing."

"Do you have a name for this person, Doctor?"

"Oh, let me see, Derek, David, Dermot, eh… wait now, no, Damian, yes that was it. Damian."

"Do you have a surname? Where did he come from?"

"Oh, no, sorry. It was just a cash in hand arrangement, I'm afraid. I never knew his surname, or his address."

"How did he contact you initially?"

"I think he just knocked at the door. The place must have been looking a bit scruffy. I've no time for gardening, I'm afraid."

"It looks immaculate just now. Does Damian still look after it?"

"No, no, we haven't seen him in ages. We hire a firm of professional landscapers now. They come once a week. It's a much better set up. They are totally reliable, and not much more expensive, and of course it's legitimate – they are fully insured, and charge VAT et cetera."

"Do you know if this Damian did any work for anyone else on the road?"

"No, I'm afraid not. But you could ask."

"Well, thank you very much, Doctor, you've been most helpful. I'll leave you to it now."

Willoughby showed Moore out through the surgery entrance, and said goodbye. When she was back out on the road, Moore called to a few of the houses on either side of Dr Willoughby's, but none of the occupants recognised her e-fit, and none admitted to having used Damian to tend to their gardens either, or in any other capacity.

Chapter Twenty

Friday was a fine but somewhat blustery day when Damian drove his old Nissan down along Corbawn Lane. He parked a little more than halfway down the road, not wishing anyone from Braemore House to see it, and keen to avoid capture of the vehicle on any CCTV that might be concealed around the property.

He had dressed smartly for his encounter with Mr McKinley, who had told him on the phone that while the home was fully occupied at present, his elderly relative could join a short waiting list, and would probably be able to move there within a month or two.

Before going in through the gates to Braemore House, Damian spent several minutes looking around outside the property. He could easily see into the place from the road, as there was only a small bramble hedge between the thoroughfare and the premises itself. The original house had been extended to the rear, and a modern looking two-storey block that obviously accommodated private rooms stuck out on two sides with a courtyard in the centre. There was a galvanized metal stair leading down from an emergency exit at the end of both of the two blocks – an arrangement Damian had become used to in the recent past. Several PIR activated floodlights pointed downwards into the courtyard.

Beyond this, well-manicured lawns led away to the boundary and he could see that the back of the extensive plot faced onto a row of detached houses with good-sized back gardens. There was a six-foot high concrete wall separating them from the old people's home, which would limit his escape route in the event that one was needed. The front of the home, as described on its website, terminated at the edge of a sheer drop down to Shankill beach. But outside the gates, there was a small, rough path, that also zig-zagged down to the beach, although descending it would be difficult, and coming up would be a nightmare. Damian spent a few minutes examining the arrangement.

He then went into the grounds of the place, and had to admit that it was beautifully maintained and enjoyed magnificent views out to the slightly choppy waters of the Irish Sea where the waves were topped with white horses.

At the entrance to the property, a rather corpulent security guard dressed in a black uniform complete with a peaked cap sat at a small desk which had been placed in the porch where it looked totally makeshift, but nevertheless served its purpose.

Damian greeted the man with his best smile, "Hello there. I have an appointment with Mr McKinley. I'm coming to look over the place for my father."

"That's fine. If I could just have your name please?" the security guard said raising his ballpoint pen to write in the hard-backed journal that rested on his desk.

"Yes, of course. I'm Jeremy, Jeremy Shanahan," Damian said.

"Thank you, Mr Shanahan. I'll just let Mr McKinley know you are here," the man said getting up from his position and side-stepping awkwardly around the desk before disappearing inside the building. While he was gone, Damian scanned the guard's notebook and saw that there had been just three other visitors to the place that day, one of them being identified as 'Electrician'.

A moment later the security guard re-emerged and took his place behind the desk again. He was followed by a distinguished-looking man in his fifties dressed in cavalry twill trousers, and a thin maroon pullover topped off with a classic Harris tweed jacket complete with leather elbow patches. The man's check shirt was open at the neck, but still managed to portray an image of some elegance.

"Good afternoon, Mr Shanahan. Thank you for coming," McKinley said in an educated but nondescript accent as he held out his hand to greet Damian.

"Hello, Mr McKinley. It's a beautiful place you have here. A lovely location, if I may say so."

"Thank you. Yes, we chose it largely for the location. It's quite unique. But please, come inside. Can I arrange some refreshments?"

"No thanks. I'm not long after my lunch. So, how many residents do you have here?" Damian said.

"Twenty-five at the moment. They are nearly all singles, but we have one couple who share a suite at the back. They've been married for nearly sixty years, you know."

McKinley was now walking down along the hall, and turned to face Damian, gesturing him to go into a sort of office. Damian noted that the whole place smelled of polish and fresh flowers – not like the abominable stench of pee that he often encountered in these places. All of the paintwork was fresh and the place was spotlessly clean.

Damian took a seat in front of the mahogany desk where McKinley sat, and waited for the proprietor to speak.

"Well now, you said on the phone that you wanted to discuss arrangements for your father, is that right, Mr Shanahan?"

"Yes, that's right."

"May I ask how old he is?"

Damian was not prepared for this question, but hoped that it didn't show. He replied promptly enough in any case.

"Eh, seventy-six next birthday he'll be."

"And is he in good health?"

"Mostly. He has a bit of arthritis, but he's still mobile, even if he has to use a stick from time to time. Especially in damp weather," Damian said.

"I see. And does he have his own doctor, or would he need to be enrolled with our man here?"

"I'm not sure, but I can ask him, if we proceed with the arrangements."

"Ah, yes, I see. You are a discerning man, Mr Shanahan. Why don't we have a look around and then if you're happy with what you see, I can give you an application form before you leave."

Damian was treated to an extensive tour of the premises that lasted a full half-hour, before the two men returned to the office.

"Well. What do you think?"

"Very nice. Dad could be comfortable here. But you said that your residents are largely made up of academics and the like. Have you anyone famous with you at all?"

"Well, not really famous. There is Cynthia Dunne of course. Mrs Dunne held the chair in Biosciences at Trinity long before it was called that. She is, or was, one of the world's leading experts on child immunisation, or so she tells me. She's been published several times, and has worked in various African countries in the past. We've given her that nice room on the ground floor with a view out across the gardens to the sea."

"I see. My father's mind is very active. He loves to keep occupied mentally."

"Then he'll be coming to the right place. We have a strong focus on keeping everyone here in good mental order."

"And what about security at Braemore House, Mr McKinley? You hear such dreadful things these days about retirement homes. I'd need to know that dad is safe."

"Oh, you need have no worries on that score. Since these, eh, incidents, we have hired a full-time security guard. You may have seen him on your way in. And it's a 24-7 arrangement. The night man comes on at eight o'clock and does twelve hours. And, of course we have CCTV all around the perimeter of the house as well. He'll be perfectly safe here, you need have no worries in that regard."

"I see. That all sounds very thorough. Does the night man, as you call him, patrol the grounds or does he stay indoors?" Damian asked.

"No, he stays indoors, and keeps watch using the CCTV system."

"I see."

Damian felt he could make no further enquiries about the security at the place for fear of arousing suspicion, so he left it at that.

McKinley finished the encounter by giving Damian a four-page application form and asking when, approximately, did Damian think his father would be ready to move in.

Damian dodged the question, and told McKinley that he had one or two more places to see, adding, "But I don't think any of them will be as nice as this. Thank you very much for showing me around."

As he walked back up the road to his car, he muttered, "Excellent – just what I needed to know. Thanks, McKinley!"

Chapter Twenty-One

The e-fit of Damian adorned the front pages of all the daily newspapers the following morning. 'Have you seen this man?' rang out the bold headline, together with details of a phone number to contact in case the response was affirmative. The Gardaí had set up a small team of civilian workers to field the incoming calls, and as usual, the phones were hopping with alleged sightings coming in from all over the country. Each one had to be followed up, although the more unlikely ones – 'That's a perfect match for our local councillor' insisted a caller from Kerry in the far south-west of the country – were given short shrift.

"Anything happening on the phones?" Burke asked Moore as they got together to assess progress – or lack of it.

"Just the usual. They're up to over two hundred calls already, but nothing useful. I have Dónal on standby in case anything positive comes in. Sometimes I wonder if these sorts of things are worth it," Moore said.

"Me too, but at least we are seen to be doing something. This thing is doing my head in. We appear to be completely at the mercy of this gouger. All we can do is wait for him to strike for the fourth time," Burke said.

"Let's get everyone together and go over what we do know again. We may have missed something significant along the way. What do you think?"

"Yes, OK. It's better than sitting here twiddling our thumbs anyway."

Moore summoned their small team to the open plan, asking Séan Reilly to organise coffees for them on his way in.

She stood at the top of the room close to the whiteboard that carried pictures of the victims and of course a copy of the e-fit, along with the name of Dr Fleming and the proprietors of the homes where the crimes had been committed.

"OK, folks. Let's go over exactly what we have so far. We need to make some progress with this – and soon," she said. "Let's start with forensics. Dónal – what have we?"

"I've got the soil analysis we lifted from the shoe print in Vico View back now, boss. Most of the soil was from the base of the fire escape where he gained entry, but there were traces of another type of soil too. Unfortunately, it's not particularly rare, but they were able to eliminate any coastal location, and said it was a common type found in many areas of the southside of the city and suburbs."

"Great! Not much help then. Anything else?"

"Yes. The forensic people examining the footprint say there's an unusual wear pattern on the left sole. They are going to see if they can get hold of a forensic podiatrist to see what they can make of it. It could be chummy has some problem with his leg, or maybe even a slight limp. Oh, and they're fairly happy that the morphine that was found at Cedar Hill came from the batch stolen from Dr Willoughby's," Lawler said.

"How many phials were in that lot?" More asked.

"Five, boss."

Moore rolled her eyes to heaven.

"Are you thinking what I'm thinking?" Lawler said.

"Two more to go, you mean?"

"Exactly!"

"OK, Séan, have you anything more from that software you've been playing with?"

"I've put all the most up to date information into it, boss. And I ran another two thousand passes last night. It says there's a fifteen to twenty percent chance that there's some kind of educational connection, based on all the information we put in. And our friend is almost certainly a part-time worker – like as not works outdoors. I'll input that new information about his feet and see if it highlights anything more."

"Well I could have told you most of that myself, Séan, but thanks anyway. Talk to the team manning the phones and see if you can get any more nuggets to feed your new toy with."

"What about the first victim, and more particularly, her family – Humphries, was it?" Burke said, looking at the whiteboard for confirmation. "I wasn't too happy about that son of hers, the insurance bloke, and you know what I think when there's money involved."

"Do you want us to go and have another chat with him, sir?" Lawler asked.

"Might be no harm, though I can't see any connection to the subsequent killings, unless Séan's miracle machine can come up with something. Séan – can you ask that thing about insurances. Find out if there were any life policies or anything that might be connected to Humphries, or even household insurance for any of the other victims. He could be on the fiddle if he's under pressure for money."

"OK, but it isn't suggesting any connection between the victims at all, except that they were all old ladies and living in old peoples' homes," Reilly said.

"Just check it for me, will you?" Burke said, slightly irritated by the young man's reluctance.

"Right, that's all for now. Fiona, you and I are going to put our heads together and do some detecting. OK?"

"Yes, sure, sir."

* * *

Burke and Moore went into Burke's office and sat down.

"Right, Fiona, let's harness our joint deductive powers and see if we can outsmart that infernal machine. Give me some questions," Burke said.

"OK. Well, first up, why all women? I know there are more of them in these places than men, but there were a good few men in the Dartry one."

"Physical strength, maybe. Perhaps our man is diminutive and not very strong, so women are easier to overcome if things get rough," Burke said.

"Hmm... maybe. I'm not convinced though. These old geezers in these places are pretty feeble. And why just the southside?"

"That's easier. He lives somewhere there. If you connect the dots between Glenageary, Dartry and Dalkey/Killiney, what do you get?"

"It puts him somewhere in the Cabinteely, Cornelscourt area. But hold on – that's not it," Moore said.

"How do you mean?"

"Look at the map. It's the roads. He needs to be able to get away quickly afterwards, so he stays close to main roads. And Dr Coogan says he probably lives in a grotty flat or bedsit somewhere. You won't find any of them in Cabinteely, it's much too up-market."

"So?" Burke said.

"So, look at the map again. Where do all the roads out of these places lead, where you might find grotty bedsits?"

"I dunno. Let's see. Ringsend, maybe? Irishtown? Pearse Street, perhaps?"

"Exactly! I reckon he lives in this area," Moore said drawing a circle on the map bounded by Sandymount

Village, Shelbourne Road, Pearse Street, Ringsend and back to Sandymount again.

"Nice one, Sergeant. Level of certainty?" Burke said.

"I'll deny this if you ever quote it back – but I'd say sixty percent."

"Good enough for me," Burke said reaching for the phone.

"Who are you calling?" Moore said.

"Detective Inspector Jim Mulcahy. He works in Irishtown Garda Station. I have known him for years."

Moore remained quiet until Burke got through to his mate in Irishtown Garda station which was located at the end of Londonbridge Road at the junction of Tritonville Road, right on the edge of Moore's target area.

When Burke had exchanged pleasantries with Mulcahy, he got down to business. He explained their involvement with the murders in the old peoples' homes, which of course Mulcahy was fully familiar with.

"So, how can I help, Aidan?" Mulcahy said.

"We think chummy may live somewhere on your patch. Our profiler says he's a loner who probably lives in a grotty bedsit or small flat somewhere, and my sergeant has a theory that he's holed up somewhere around Ringsend or Irishtown."

"I see. Any evidence to support this theory?"

"Nothing concrete, but I'm inclined to go along with her, all the same."

"OK. So, what do you want me to do?" Mulcahy said.

"Any chance you could set up a few checkpoints? You know, pretend you're just checking for tax and insurance, but make sure the Gardaí manning the stops are familiar with the e-fit and description."

"Hmm... I suppose we could put up one or two in the area. Move them around a bit to get more coverage. Have you any information on his vehicle type?"

"No, 'fraid not. But I doubt if it's this year's BMW or Mercedes!"

"OK, Aidan. Let me get on and set this up for you. I'll let you know if we get anything."

"Thanks, Jim. Much obliged."

When Burke had finished the call, he said to Moore, "Jim is sound. He'll do more than he said on the call, but it's still an awfully long shot."

"I know. But we're due some kind of break, don't you agree?"

"It doesn't always work like that, Sergeant. We'll see."

* * *

By the end of the day, close to four hundred phone calls had been taken by the team in response to the media appeal. Almost all were rubbish, but uniformed Gardaí had been despatched to check out three men that could possibly have some questions to answer. Each had proved to be honest, hard-working individuals who all had solid alibis for the dates and times of the crimes, so as evening drew in, the Garda were no further on.

Chapter Twenty-Two

When Damian returned from Shankill he was elated. He had already decided that he would definitely target Braemore House, and that Cynthia Dunne would be his next victim. He was relishing the challenge of getting into the home and seeing the old woman off – especially now that there was a full-time security presence there. He would show them that such measures were no deterrent to an accomplished killer such as he. He didn't like that smug McKinley character either, and in any case, he still had two phials of morphine that he wanted to use up.

He needed to get another couple of hypodermic syringes. He had discarded the last one he used in a huge green wheelie bin up at the school where he worked, rinsing it out to remove the traces of the morphine and making sure that it was wiped clean of any fingerprints before dumping it.

He would go to the chemist at the top of Bath Avenue and buy another one, or two if he could get away with it, explaining that he needed them to treat woodworm in some old furniture. That's how he had got the other ones, though of course in a different pharmacy. It always seemed to work, and he would go in wearing overalls, as if to emphasise his status as a woodworker.

***

Damian stopped his car the following morning at the top of Bath Avenue and parked outside the Spar shop. There were double yellow lines on the road, but everyone ignored them and left their cars there for a few minutes while they popped in for some instant groceries, or a sandwich and a coffee.

The pharmacy opposite was a brightly lit affair and looked to be part of some chain or other. It had recently been revamped, and now sported automatic doors, as well as a huge plate glass window displaying all sorts of lotions and potions to help make women look younger, or at least to 'prevent premature ageing', or so they claimed. Photographs of pretty girls in their twenties were scattered about as if to make the point, although it would be several years, perhaps decades, before these gorgeous models would even have to think about wrinkles or crows' feet.

Inside, an equally pretty girl with long blonde hair, dressed in a grey tunic the colour of which matched the paintwork of the premises almost exactly, greeted Damian with a broad smile, showing off a mouthful of unnaturally white, straight teeth.

Damian explained his requirement, and the girl went behind the display units to consult with the pharmacist – a miserable-looking man in his mid-fifties with short hair, wrinkled skin, and a mean, narrow, cheerless expression who was dressed in a white lab coat.

She re-appeared a few moments later with two hypodermic needles, each wrapped in cellophane packets, and put them into a paper bag.

"Be careful how you dispose of them, sir. They can be dangerous," the girl said, offering them to Damian and quoting the price of eight euro which Damian tendered exactly in cash.

"Thank you," he muttered, and left the shop.

Damian placed the paper bag carefully in the glove compartment of his old Nissan and travelled on to the school where he worked. He would be in late, but no one really watched what time he arrived or left, and at this stage he had prioritized his next rendezvous with death over his work in any case.

He spent the day ticking off one or two small jobs on the secretary's endless list of tasks. There was a broken window in one of the old classrooms. Not an uncommon occurrence, and one that was easily remedied. He was a regular customer in the local glaziers, and once he had taken the measurements carefully, he went there and purchased a replacement which he installed, making the place as good as new.

Damian spent his lunch break planning his next escapade. It would be Friday – being his day off, he would have plenty of time to prepare everything properly, although, in fairness, he thought to himself, these executions were all too easy. There might be a bit more security at Braemore House than he was used to, but he felt sure that the issue could be dealt with easily enough. If it was a nice day, he would travel out to Shankill during the afternoon and do a proper reconnaissance of the place. There would be other people about enjoying the view, and perhaps even swimming off the beach, so he would mix in readily with the crowd. Then he would drive on into Bray and have fish and chips on the seafront. He would walk the promenade to fill in the time before returning to Corbawn Lane sometime after ten o'clock to carry out his mission.

* * *

Friday was exactly as he had hoped it would be. It was warm and dry, and the weather forecast was predicting temperatures in the mid-twenties for the afternoon with no cloud to speak of all along the east coast.

Damian rose at soon after nine, and when he had breakfasted and washed himself, he set about his preparations. Donning a pair of black nitrile gloves – one of several pairs he had taken from the plentiful supply at the school – he removed one of the hypodermic syringes from its packaging and carefully filled it with the entire contents of a single phial of morphine. He put the little plastic cap back over the open end of the syringe to make sure that none of the liquid escaped, and then placed it along with the needle, still protected by its own plastic covering, into a clear plastic tube with a red stopper. He wasn't going to take the morphine container with him as he had done on the first caper. That was a bad mistake, but apparently of no consequence, as no one had come knocking on his door since, so he had been lucky to get away with it.

By lunchtime, Damian was feeling restless, so he changed into a pair of stone-coloured lightweight jeans and donned a maroon polo shirt and prepared to leave. He carefully placed his weapon of choice into his dark blue overalls, and folded them over, putting them into a plastic supermarket bag that he would place in the boot of the car.

As Damian drove out onto Shelbourne Road, he was stopped by a Garda checkpoint just before the junction of Lansdowne Road. The Garda gave the various pieces of official paper stuck to his windscreen a cursory glance, and then waved him on without talking to him. There was quite a traffic jam built up behind the checkpoint, and obviously the Gardaí didn't want to delay people unnecessarily.

When he arrived at his destination, he drove down along Corbawn Lane until he met a large cluster of cars parked on both sides of the narrow road, near the entrance to the steep path down to the beach. He had been right. The place was fairly crowded, which would provide him with the cover he needed for his observations. He parked, and walked down along the road towards Braemore House. As he approached the entrance, he noticed that one of the parked cars was in fact a Garda car. Inside, a young constable and his pretty female colleague were enjoying a sandwich and a take-away coffee apiece, with the windows of the vehicle wound down.

Damian wondered how long they would be there, but calculated that they would hardly remain on duty late on into the evening. After all, if nothing else, their shift would change at around tea-time. He needn't have worried. As he strolled around trying to look purposeful, the Garda car started up and departed.

Damian continued his reconnaissance of Braemore House. Looking in through the gates, he could see the security man seated at his station in the porch. He had his jacket off, and large damp patches were showing on his plain white shirt under his armpits. He was clearly uncomfortable, and in poor physical condition. He wondered if he should venture in and engage the man in conversation. He needed to get a better look at the back of the premises to see how he might gain entry later on, but mindful that he could encounter Mr McKinley again, he decided against this course of action. Instead, Damian walked around to the row of houses that backed onto Braemore House. There were several whose back gardens adjoined the grounds of the retirement home, and Damian observed that one of the properties looked to be completely unoccupied. There were no curtains visible, and when he got closer, he could see that there was no furniture in the long lounge that went from front to back of the house.

Seeing no sign of anyone in either of the adjoining houses, Damian went into the front garden and tried the side gate that gave access to the rear garden. It was open. He carried on, walking down along the narrow concrete path to the end of the garden where he could stand on an old plastic crate that was left lying there and look over into the grounds of Braemore House. He studied the layout for a few minutes, and then retreated hastily back the way he had come. He didn't think he had been spotted, and in any case, he had a reasonable story ready if anyone challenged him.

Satisfied that he now had a plan for later, he returned to his car and drove on into Bray where he enjoyed a tasty fish supper from one of the many fish and chip shops dotted along the sea front.

Chapter Twenty-Three

Moore wasn't happy – not happy at all. Burke was right – they were getting nowhere with the case, and with the AC breathing down their necks, it was doing them no good at all. This fella was making them look like amateurs. As the office thinned out for the evening, she asked Séan Reilly if he wouldn't mind staying back for a few minutes to go over some of the stuff that he had put into the AccuDet software.

Séan was a young, enthusiastic civilian worker whose family came from deep in rural Ireland close to Kilkenny. His father was a small farmer. That is to say, he owned and operated a small farm, not that he was small in stature – far from it. Together with his wife, Blanad, they had produced three children, two boys and a girl. Séan was the youngest, and in the Irish tradition, not being in line to inherit the farm, he had to seek work elsewhere once he had finished schooling. In an earlier era, he might have signed up for the priesthood, but recruitment for the church had slowed to a trickle in recent times, and so Séan found himself enrolling in the Civil Service. During his training, he discovered that he had a knack with computers. The rather modest technology at the training college was constantly in need of attention, and Séan was often called to help sort out knotty technical issues, which he seemed to be able to accomplish with consummate ease. He had no formal training in the discipline, but he certainly had a natural flair, and so when he graduated from training he was assigned to the Garda Technical Bureau where he continued to enhance his knowledge of all things electronic.

He had been drafted into Store Street Garda station almost by accident. The station was light-handed, and Séan was getting a bit bored, constantly having to show inexperienced users how to perform trivial tasks on their equipment, so he had volunteered for a transfer to Store Street where he felt he would be exposed to some 'real' policing. He wasn't wrong.

"I want to go over everything that's been put into this thing, Séan. Can you give me the five-penny tour?" Moore said, sitting down alongside the lad in a corner of the open plan.

"Sure, Sarge," Séan responded, pleased to have the opportunity to demonstrate his skills with the application.

When he had shown Moore around the profile that had been created of their perpetrator, Moore sat back.

"So, chummy knows his way around locks and fire escapes, possibly works outdoors, had some general handyman skills. He also has limp, or some defect in his gait, and he possibly lives in a rather downbeat area of town and has a car, or at least the use of one. Does that more or less sum up what we know?" Moore said.

"Not quite, boss. He knows how to give an injection too. The women that he filled with morphine weren't handled roughly. The pathologist said he was gentle with them, apart from smothering them, of course."

"Hmm... OK. So, what does that tell us, Séan?"

"Maybe he has cared for an elderly relative at some stage – someone who needed regular injections, or perhaps he's diabetic and has to inject himself daily?"

"Excellent! Your software didn't tell you that, now did it?" Moore said a little smugly.

"Eh, no. But it might have done if I'd put that information in. It's my fault really."

"AccuDet says he only works part-time, or to be more precise, only four days a week. He seems to have Fridays off. That's when he tended to the doctor's garden, and it's the day that the killings have taken place too."

"Right. Can you bring up a map of the Ringsend area on that thing?" Moore said.

Reilly fiddled with the computer for a moment and the screen filled with Google Maps showing the area that they were interested in.

"Now, let's see how many parks and open spaces there are close to where we think he lives. Look – there's Herbert Park, Lansdowne Road, the hockey pitches at Londonbridge Road, Merrion Cricket Club and a bit further out Wanderers and of course Donnybrook. Tomorrow morning, can you get onto all of those places and see if they employ any groundsmen or handymen Monday to Thursday only, and if so get details?"

"Yes, OK. What about schools?"

"Oh yes, you're right. Let's have another look at the map. See – there are several schools in the area with grounds attached – you'd better check them out as well. Did we get anything back from the checkpoints?"

"No, nothing. But to be fair, they don't really know what they are looking for, boss."

"I suppose you're right. But we need to find a way to ID this guy. His car would do it, or anything else he was careless about. Is there anything more – anything at all – you can get out of this thing?" Moore said, pointing to Reilley's PC.

"Not unless I can get more data points to enter into it. I've done thousands of runs and it's given all it has to give with what it's got so far."

"OK. Well, let me know immediately if you get a hit tomorrow on your ring around the parks and sports grounds."

Back at her desk, Moore was still restless. She took out a list of the care homes that they had downloaded earlier and studied it. The southside of Dublin was littered with them. Many of them were small undertakings housing between ten and twenty residents, but there was the occasional larger undertaking too where up to a hundred retirees spent their twilight years.

She studied the list hoping for some inspiration. She was looking for anything in common between the premises that he had already targeted; some thread that would give her a clue to where his next victim was to be found.

One after another, she brought up the websites of the homes from the list. She felt he was more likely to go for the smaller ones, especially now that the authorities had their guard up. The bigger ones would have installed heavy security, not wanting any of their residents to fall victim. One by one she eliminated several of the facilities, but there were still a large number left.

Then she looked closely at the location of each of the homes that remained. Even the place in Dartry, which was in quite a built-up area, was secluded. It had extensive grounds that allowed their man quite good cover. Cedar Hill and Vico View were the same. So Moore struck out any of the homes that opened onto a busy thoroughfare, or were heavily overlooked by other properties. The list was getting smaller.

It was just after seven o'clock when Moore had finished whittling down the list of nursing homes, using, what she had to admit, was somewhat unscientific methods. But there was nothing for her at home anyway except a reheated frozen dinner and the dregs of a bottle of mediocre red wine, so she took the list and decided to do a tour of the premises that were left on it. The rush hour traffic had subsided by this time, so it would only take her an hour or two to nip around to them all and see if she could get some inspiration.

* * *

As she set out from the city centre, Moore pointed the car southwards. She was soon in Ballsbridge, and she turned right off the Merrion Road into Ailesbury Road. There was just one retirement home on this road, and as she approached it, she noticed that security appeared to be very tight. The tall wrought iron gates were closed, and anyone hoping to enter would have to ring the bell and be invited in. A thick, tall, prickly hedge surrounded the front of the property, and the black-panelled front door was firmly closed. It was hard to see how any casual caller could gain access easily, so Moore moved on.

The next few homes she passed were similarly well protected. It wasn't till she got to Dún Laoghaire that things changed. Clarinda Park was a square of terraced three-storey houses. The properties looked over a large cultivated square with railings all around, which substituted for front gardens, as each house had just a small patch of ground between the foot of its granite steps and the footpath. On one side of the square, three of these houses had been conjoined to create a spacious and relatively elegant retirement home. The front door of the leftmost house of the three stood open, with just an inner glazed porch door between the outside world and the home itself.

Moore parked her car and got out. She climbed the steps up to the open door and rang the bell. After waiting for several minutes during which there was no response, she tried the round brass handle on the inner door which opened easily, admitting her into the tiled hallway of the house. Inside, there was still no sign of anyone, but she could hear the noise of voices coming from a room deep within. Moore advanced along the corridor towards the back of the premises and called, "Hello, is anyone there?"

With still no response, she located the room from where the noise of voices was coming. Inside the room were several elderly residents, most of whom were watching TV, but one old lady had ear plugs in and was reading a Kindle. None of the occupants paid any attention as Moore came in, and there appeared to be no carers present, so she left again and continued on down the corridor to the very back of the house where a kitchen was located. As she entered, two women clad in green nurses' uniforms looked up startled. In front of both of them were large glasses of clear liquid, and a vodka bottle, more than half empty, stood open nearby.

"Which of you is in charge?" Moore demanded.

The two women looked at each other for a moment, and then the one sitting nearest to where Moore was standing said, "We both are. Why? Who wants to know?"

Moore pulled her warrant card from her jacket pocket and introduced herself.

"Do you two realise that I've been in this house for several minutes? I just walked in off the street. No one challenged me, and there appears to be no security of any kind here. What's going on?"

This time, the second woman piped up.

"Nothing's going on. The patients are all watching TV. They have a bell if they need us. We've been running around all day, so we've just sat down to relax for a few minutes."

Moore walked further into the room.

"Are you two aware that a number of people have been murdered in old peoples' homes around here in the recent past? Someone got in and smothered them. And here you are, leaving the place wide open to the four winds with not a care in the world. Who owns this place?"

The two women looked at each other nervously.

"A Mrs Ryan but she's away on holiday in America this week."

"I need her phone number, full name and address."

Neither of the women moved, and Moore's patience was running out.

"Now would be good!" she said sternly, and finally one of the women stood up and made her way to a dresser at the side of the room and handed a business card to Moore.

"Get this place secured immediately. Then check all the rooms to make sure there's no one here that shouldn't be. Make certain the back entrance is locked up too. Who's on duty overnight?"

"No one. Mrs Ryan wouldn't pay for a night nurse. There's a number they can phone if anyone is in trouble and a doctor will come."

"And how would the doctor get in?" Moore said.

"He has a key, hasn't he?" one of the women said cheekily.

"Right, well I'm going to try and arrange for a uniformed Garda to come up and stay here till more permanent arrangements can be made. You'll have to stay until he gets here. I presume that won't be a problem?"

The women looked at each other again, and mumbled their assent.

"And put that bloody vodka away, for God's sake."

As Moore went back to her car, she called Dún Laoghaire Garda station and made the arrangements, quoting the AC to bypass any possible objections.

Then she travelled on, up through Mountown, and into Glenageary. She stopped outside Cedar Hill, and was pleased to note that the premises was now secure, and a set of new CCTV cameras had been installed at various points around the perimeter. Notices from a well-known security company advised callers that they should report to reception, and that trespassers would be prosecuted.

"Well, at least someone is getting the message," she said to herself as she drove off to the next location.

Chapter Twenty-Four

It was after ten o'clock when Damian returned to Corbawn Lane. The trippers had gone, but there was a surprising number of cars parked on the narrow road all the same. He found a spot well up from Braemore House, and just managed to squeeze his old car into the space, although the front end of the vehicle ended up partially blocking a driveway.

"There won't be anyone going out at this hour," he reassured himself, "it will be grand."

Damian went to the boot of his car and raised the lid with a loud creak from the rusty old hinges. He donned a pair of nitrile gloves and collected a plastic supermarket bag full of rag waste that he had taken from the school, and poured an entire litre of paraffin oil into it. He winced slightly at the strong smell from the liquid, but it was soon absorbed by the old cloths in the bag. He closed the boot of the car as silently as he could manage, and set off on foot down the road.

It was nearly dark, but not yet pitch black when he got to the gates of the place, which were thankfully wide open. Damian had a look around to ensure that he was not being observed, and slipped in, staying close to the rhododendron bushes to the left of the entrance. He could see from this vantage point that the doors of the home had not yet been sealed for the night, and the corpulent security man was still seated at his position in the porch with a mug of something in front of him as he ate a sandwich.

Damian reached into the pocket of his dark overalls which now covered his brightly coloured outfit, and took out the little gas cigarette lighter. He fired it up, and touched it against a piece of soaking cloth in the top of the bag. It caught immediately, and the fire spread quite quickly through the impregnated material. Before it became too much for Damian to handle, he threw the bag through the air as far as he could manage towards the end of the garden that faced out onto the beach. The flaming missile looked bizarre arcing high above the manicured lawn, before it landed in a fiery mess on the grass some fifteen feet from the garden's edge.

The security man saw the fireball as it travelled on its trajectory, and with his mouth still full of sandwich, let out a yelp while standing up suddenly and spilling his drink all over himself and the floor.

"Damn!" he exclaimed, and he lumbered across the grass towards the conflagration, without any plan for what he might do with it when he got there.

With the door to the property now completely unguarded, Damian slipped in and hid himself in an alcove in the hallway, straining to hear the sounds that would evidence the presence of people, and give him information as to where they were. But the entire property seemed to be in total silence, which, as far as Damian was concerned, was a good thing. It looked as if the inmates had retired for the night. Excellent, he thought.

With the security man still engaged with the fire in the garden – he was stamping ineffectively at the burning fragments at the edge of where the bag had melted down – Damian moved to the door of Cynthia Dunne's room which Mr McKinley had so kindly identified for him during his earlier visit.

He slipped quietly into the room and quickly orientated himself. The curtains were not very heavy, and a good amount of light was still coming in. He could see the flickering of the flames from his diversion still going strong out in the garden. Damian withdrew the syringe from his pocket, and removed the cap protecting the sharp end of the needle, making sure to put it away carefully. He then approached the bed where Mrs Dunne appeared to be asleep, lying on her back, with her right arm conveniently placed outside the covers, exposing the veins in her forearm.

Damian leaned in, syringe at the ready, to deliver his deadly dose, and as he bent over the prone form of the woman, she quickly turned, and bringing her left hand rapidly out from under the covers, whacked him on the side of the head with a stout piece of polished mahogany she had previously removed from an item of furniture.

Mayhem ensued. Mrs Dunne started screaming at the top of her voice. She was out of the bed in an instant, and with Damian still reeling from the first blow, she whacked him another two times with all her strength.

But Damian was not one to give in easily, though his thoughts now turned to escape, abandoning his intended mission. He staggered to his feet, holding the side of his head which had started to bleed a little, grabbed Mrs Dunne by the arms, threw her roughly on the bed and made off through the door of the room which he had left ajar.

Hearing the kerfuffle, the security man left the fire, and was lumbering back towards the house when Damian emerged through the front door. The man gave chase, and despite his obvious lack of fitness, managed to pursue Damian out through the front gates, shouting loudly for him to stop.

Damian was dizzy, and just managing to stay upright, and ahead of his pursuer. He emerged onto Corbawn Lane, and decided that his best means of escape would be to descend the steep path to the beach. He doubted that the man following him would be fit enough to follow him, and he was right.

Seeing Damian disappear over the cliff, the security man ran back to Braemore House and raised the alarm. He had a panic button near to his station at the front door, and he pressed it firmly, sending an immediate signal directly to Shankill Garda station, where an alert young Garda wasted no time in taking action.

* * *

Moore was less than a mile away when she heard the call coming through on the radio. She had continued her patrol of the nursing homes, and her journey had led her to Rathmichael – an upmarket suburb on the west side of the main Wicklow road, not far from Loughlinstown.

"All units, all units. Suspected attack at Braemore House on Corbawn Lane. Suspect has made off on foot. Urgent assistance required."

She put on her blue lights, and sped as quickly as she could manage to the end of Corbawn Lane, arriving at the same time as two squad cars with a pair of Gardaí in each. She ran into the home, where the distraught security guard told his rather embarrassing story.

"I followed him as best I could, Miss, but he was too quick for me. He's gone down onto the beach."

"Is anybody here hurt?" Moore said.

"Mrs Dunne is a bit shook up, but she's OK. There's a nurse with her now. She says she gave him a good battering before he ran off."

Moore said to the two nimblest of the Gardaí that had arrived, "Right, you two with me." And turning to the other two less agile members of the force she said, "You two stay here and sort this out. Get forensics here, and see if there's a dog unit available."

Moore, accompanied by her two colleagues, trotted back out of the premises and went to the path that led down to the beach.

"I'll go first," she said, and without waiting for a reply, she started to scramble down the steep incline leading to the beach some 30 feet below. On the way down, she caught her clothes on brambles that had grown over the narrow path in places, and as she neared the beach, nettles stung her ankles which were now exposed.

Once on the beach itself it was easy to follow the footsteps that led away in the soft shingle. Damian had turned left at the base of the cliff and the three Gardaí had no difficulty tracking their quarry for several hundred yards along the sand. But then things changed. The land sloped gently down to sea level and after about 500 metres, the back gardens of modern houses were more or less level with the beach. Here, the footprints stopped abruptly, bringing the trio to a halt as well.

Moore got on her radio and asked if there was any sign of the dog unit she had requested.

"They're on their way, Sarge. Should be here in about ten minutes."

* * *

When Damian managed to shake off the security guard, he had more or less tumbled down the rough path leading from the end of the lane to the beach. When he landed at the bottom, his dodgy leg was paining him badly, and the wounds in his head were beginning to throb, blurring his vision and giving him a massive headache.

He had jogged and stumbled along the beach, not knowing if he was going to collapse at any moment, until he arrived at the back gardens of a row of houses that backed onto the sea. There was just a low wall separating the properties from the beach, and he scrambled over into one of them. The house was in darkness, and he made his way to the rear of the property, opened the side gate, and slipped out through the front onto the road.

He wasn't sure exactly where he was, but he calculated he couldn't be more than a few hundred metres from the lane where he had parked his car. But he was confused from the bangs on the head, and at first, he set off in completely the wrong direction, having to retrace his steps a few minutes later when he realised his error.

"All these damn roads look the same," he said in frustration as he tried this one and then that to see if he could get back to Corbawn Lane, and at one stage he felt as if he was going round in circles.

* * *

Moore and her two assistants were still on the beach when the dog handler arrived. He was accompanied by a beautiful black and sable German shepherd called Jack. Jack had bright eyes, a wet nose and pointed ears, and was in full pursuit mode by the time he reached the spot where the three were standing. His handler, Garda McMullen, introduced them both. "Sergeant, do you mind if we get on with this. If he's still on foot, our best chance is to get going, isn't that right, boy," he said patting the anxious hound on his head.

"Go for it!" Moore replied, and McMullen and Jack clambered over the wall into the back garden of the house where Damian had been just twenty minutes earlier. Jack kept his nose to the ground and followed a direct line to the side gate of the house, and then out onto the road. Jack and Garda McMullen followed the scent left by Damian on its meandering route, with Moore and her two colleagues bringing up the rear.

"Are you sure this is right, Guard?" Moore said, when the entourage turned back on itself and appeared to be confused. McMullen gave her a sour look and said, "Please don't distract him, Sergeant, he knows what he's doing."

"Well that's me told," Moore said under her breath.

Jack kept following the scent, bringing the Gardaí around all the roads that Damian had used, until eventually they emerged out onto Corbawn Lane. He led them up along the narrow road for a few hundred metres, and then came abruptly to a halt alongside a vacant parking space. Jack pirouetted a few times in frustration and then sat down and looked rather mournfully at his handler.

"It's OK, boy, you did your best," McMullen said by way of reassurance, but Jack was clearly disappointed not to have found his target, and lay down in the road with his head between his front paws.

"What does this mean?" Moore asked.

"He had a car parked here, Sergeant. He's away in it for sure," McMullen said.

Seeing the little group of Gardaí out on the road, the man who lived adjacent to where they were standing came out of his house.

"Good night, Guards. Can I ask what's going on?"

"We're looking for a man that may have parked his car here a bit earlier, sir. I don't suppose you noticed anything?" Moore said, extending her warrant card for the man to inspect.

"Indeed I did, bloody cheek. He only parked halfway across my drive, didn't he?"

"Did you speak to him at all, or get a good look at his face?"

"I did not. There's no point engaging with these ignorant types. They only abuse you. But I got a good look at his car. I even took a picture of it when he had gone off down the road."

"May I see please?" Moore said.

The man took an iPhone out of his trouser pocket and held it out proudly for Moore to examine. It was a sideways-on shot, but she could just make out a couple of the characters on the rear number plate.

"Just the one photo?" she said.

"Yes. A right old banger it was too."

"Could I ask you to send that to me," Moore said providing her email address so that the man could forward the picture.

"Yes, of course. But I don't want anything to do with this bloke if you do find him. What's he done anyway?"

"We're just pursuing enquiries, sir. But thank you. You have been most helpful. My colleague here will just take a note of your name, if that's OK?"

"Yes, of course. Glad to help, officer."

Moore walked away and used her radio to put out an all-points bulletin for the silver Nissan with a 'V' in the registration.

Chapter Twenty-Five

Moore thanked McMullen and Jack and sent them on their way. She then returned to Braemore House, where Andrew McKinley had arrived and was taking charge of things.

"Good evening, sir. Are you Mr McKinley?" Moore said when she saw the man's authoritative demeanour.

"I am indeed. And you are?"

Moore showed him her warrant card.

"No offence, Sergeant, but don't you think we need a more senior officer here for this? After all, one of our charges was almost murdered in her bed!"

"How is the woman, Mr McKinley?"

"She's recovering – but she got an awful fright. Did you catch the man that did it?"

"No, he seems to have got away, for now. We'll need to get a full forensic team out at once. Could you have your resident moved to another room for the moment, we need to go over the place with a fine-tooth comb? And I need to speak to the security guard as a matter of urgency."

McKinley wasn't used to taking orders, but on this occasion, he complied.

"Very well. I'll see what I can do. Sam is in the kitchen getting a cup of tea."

"Right, I'll be there in a minute."

Moore made several calls on her mobile. She firstly arranged for the forensic team to attend the premises. She managed to get hold of Phil Donnelly himself, and he said he would come out personally with several other members of the team.

"We'll be there in twenty minutes, Fiona. Try and see that the place isn't trampled on too much, and keep everyone out of the woman's room, won't you?" Donnelly said.

"Yes, thanks Phil. See you soon."

Next, she tried Burke, but his phone went to voicemail, so she just left a message for him to call her urgently. She did manage to get hold of Dónal Lawler, and he assured her that he would be there as soon as he could.

Moore then walked down the garden to where the blackened remains of Damian's fireball distraction sat in a circle of singed grass. The security man had stamped enthusiastically with his heavy boots on the fire to extinguish it, and several remnants of the rags remained – scorched, but at least partly intact.

Moore got down on her hunkers, and using a pen from her inside pocket, gently turned over some of the scraps. Within a second or two she had exposed a piece of cloth that looked like it had at one time been a towel, and there in the corner where the selvedge had prevented it from burning through, was a laundry tag. It had black letters and numbers on a small piece of striped canvas that had been attached to the towel with starch. She recognised the arrangement from the sheets her mother used to send out to be laundered when she was growing up.

Moore took a small plastic evidence bag out of her pocket, and picking the morsel of fabric up, she placed it inside the bag.

She then went in search of the security guard, who was still in the kitchen nursing a large mug of strong sugary tea.

The man's name was Sam McIvor, and he was employed by Toner Security – a small firm that provided static guards for a number of premises on the south side of the city. McIvor was originally from the North of Ireland, but had been living in Dublin for the last twelve years.

"Tell me what happened, Mr McIvor?" she said.

McIvor related the tale of how he had been on duty shortly before eleven o'clock when, all of a sudden, he saw a ball of fire landing in the bottom of the front garden.

"I didn't know what was happening, to be honest. We don't get any trouble round here normally, but I guess I just followed my instincts and went and put it out. The man must have slipped in when I was dealing with the fire. I never saw him though. God, I hope Mrs Dunne is all right. I hear she gave him what for."

By the time Moore had finished speaking to the security guard, several squad cars with uniformed Gardaí had arrived at Braemore House. She instructed one of them to take McIvor's statement when she went off in search of the intended victim.

She found the old lady in the day room, sitting in an armchair with a warm woollen rug wrapped around her. A nurse was with her, and a machine had been wheeled in to monitor the woman's vital signs to ensure that she hadn't suffered any lasting damage.

Moore pulled up a chair beside Mrs Dunne, and the nurse said to her, "Just a few questions please, officer, Mrs Dunne has had a terrible shock."

"I'm quite fine, thank you, nurse. I'm not going to let some toe rag get the better of me – damned cheek!" she said.

Mrs Dunne told Moore the story of how she had equipped herself with a rudimentary weapon when she read about the fate of the other old ladies in various homes around the southside of Dublin. She had not been asleep when her attacker came into her room, and although she was very nervous, she managed to deliver a couple of severe blows to the man's head, causing him to drop whatever he had in his hand, and run out of the room, holding the side of his head muttering expletives. She didn't get a good look at him, but she was able to give a vague description, saying that he had a round face and a dark-coloured woolly hat.

* * *

By the time Moore had finished talking to Mrs Dunne, the forensic team had arrived and were working in what had been the woman's bedroom.

"Hi Phil. Got anything yet?" she said to the senior member of the team whom she recognised, even though he was fully clad in a white suit.

"We're just getting started, but we've got the syringe. It was under the bed. And there are some smudges of blood on the door jamb. I don't think he was expecting the old woman to be so prepared for him."

"Great. And I found this outside too. It was in a plastic bag that was thrown into the garden on fire as a way of distracting the security man," Moore said.

"What is it?" Phil said, peering through the plastic bag.

"A fragment of a towel, I think. But it's got a laundry tag on it."

"Cool. We should be able to trace that handy enough. Look, I'd better get on, there's lots to do here. I'll catch you later."

"OK. Thanks, Phil."

Moore went back outside where Dónal Lawler had just arrived.

Moore briefed Lawler on the situation, and asked him to take over control of the scene.

"What are you going to do, boss?" he said.

"I want to follow up on the checkpoints – see if chummy has been spotted or better still, apprehended."

Moore then called into central control which was based in Dublin Castle. This was where the Gardaí co-ordinate efforts involving different divisions of the force, and also where all 999 calls are answered and recorded.

She got through to the night controller who told her that there had been no sightings, but that Garda in Bray had some information, and he suggested she should call them. She made the call, and spoke to a Sergeant Molloy.

"This might be nothing, Sergeant, but one of our patrol cars stopped an old silver Nissan out on the N11 about forty minutes ago. It was driving erratically, and our lads thought the driver was drunk. But he checked out OK. All his tax, insurance and so on were in order, and he hadn't been drinking. Said he was heading home to Roundwood. Your APB came in soon after, but he was long gone by that time."

"OK, thanks. Did they get the reg number?" Moore said.

"No, I'm sorry, but the Guard said he thought it was ZV something or other," Molloy said.

"Hmm... that sounds right. Thanks, Sergeant. Have you got a checkpoint organised now?"

"Oh, yes we have. In both directions. If he comes back our way, we'll have him, don't worry."

When Moore had finished the call, she sat into her own car, and thought. Moments later, she started it, and drove back up Corbawn Lane to the main Bray Road and headed south. She drove as far as the Woodbrook roundabout, and then cut up onto the N11 in the direction of Kilmacanogue. There, she took the slip road and turned on to the start of the Long Hill that would take her up to Calary Bog and on into Roundwood.

Chapter Twenty-Six

Damian had nearly lost his life when he was pulled over on the N11. He was still very agitated, and he was conscious of the wounds on his head, though fortunately they were mostly on the side away from the Garda who was leaning in through the driver's window. He could hardly believe his luck when he was waved on, and he decided that he should try and go to ground as soon as he could.

Aware that there might be further Garda activity on the route, he decided he had better go in the direction of Roundwood as he had told the Garda at the checkpoint. He needed to get some food somewhere, and hide out for a day or two to let things settle down and allow him to make some plans. It was fortunate that it was the weekend, so he didn't have to worry about missing work until Monday, and even then, he could always call in sick for a day or two without raising suspicion.

As he drove up the Long Hill he had an idea. Near the top of the hill there was an old disused quarry. It had been inactive for several years, but it was quite extensive. If he could get his car in there, he could keep it out of sight, and he could walk up the rest of the steep road to the top where a small shop and petrol station was located. He doubted if it was very well secured, so he could break in there and get some basic provisions to keep him going for a couple of days.

The fence to the old quarry was rusted and had partially collapsed, allowing Damian to drive in easily over what was left of the old chain link wire. He drove around the back of a large mound of loose gravel and, happy that the car could not be seen from the road, parked it and got out.

It was chilly now, but he soon warmed up as he set off walking on up the hill towards the shop. He encountered no one on the road, and not even one vehicle passed him as he strode on up towards his objective. At the top of the hill, the little white and red shop stood in a wide-open space with the single petrol pump outside. Although it was by now pitch dark, there was a half-moon appearing frequently from behind scurrying clouds, allowing him to see what he was about. He circled the building and could see no trace of an alarm. Round the back, a wooden door covered in a rusty steel mesh protected the rear of the shop. Damian had brought a crowbar about two feet in length with him to enable him to break in. It was shaped a bit like a hook at one end with a cloven blade, and he made short work of the flimsy hasp that was attached to the door. He pulled the door open, and was gratified that no sirens or bells started up as he entered the premises.

Inside, he collected some packets of biscuits, milk, and some tinned food as well as a good few bars of chocolate, all of which he stuffed into a plastic bag that the shopkeeper had conveniently left on the counter. He exited by the same route, and pushed the door over so that it looked as if it was closed tightly, and wandered off back down the hill to where he had hidden his car.

* * *

Moore was driving up the Long Hill, nearing the top, when her mobile phone rang. It wasn't on this occasion connected to the Bluetooth, so she decided she would have to pull in to answer it. As luck would have it, there was a convenient gap on the left-hand side of the road that looked as if it might be the entrance to an old premises of some kind. She pulled the car off the road, half in and half out of the site, and picked up the phone from the passenger's seat. She could see that it was Burke calling, but when she answered the call, the signal was breaking up really badly due to the topography of the place. She tried to have a conversation with her boss, but it was no use. Neither of them could hear the other properly, so she just managed to convey to him that she would call him back in a few minutes before she hung up.

* * *

As Damian approached his hideout coming down the hill, he saw Moore's car parked in the entrance. Although Moore's car headlights were still on, he could just make out the shape of a woman's head in the driving seat, and he could see that she was alone in the car, apparently using a mobile phone. He was certain that somehow he had been rumbled.

He quickly dumped his shopping bag in the overgrown ditch at the side of the road, and with the occupant of the car distracted with her phone, he slipped unseen along to the driver's door of Moore's car. Moore had just put her phone in her jacket pocket, and was preparing to move off when suddenly her door was ripped open, she was grabbed by her collar, and dragged out of the vehicle which, driverless, moved forward on the incline and ended up in the ditch.

As Damian dragged Moore along by her collar, she scrambled trying to no avail to establish some grip on the loose surface. She twisted her body trying to break free, but he had a good grip on her coat and he wasn't about to let her go.

Thinking quickly, Moore, now bouncing along on her backside, unzipped her jacket and wriggled out of it, leaving Damian holding an empty coat. But she was now lying on the ground on her back, and Damian was advancing on her with his iron crowbar raised high above his head menacingly.

Moore knew she had to time her next move to perfection. As the bar descended through the air towards her face, she quickly twisted her entire body away to the left, leaving the weapon to crash into the hard ground. Damian, who was still attached to the iron bar, got a nasty shock up through his arm, causing him to drop it where it rattled onto the gravel as he yelped in agony, holding his right arm with his left hand.

Moore reacted quickly. She got hold of the crowbar, and from her now sitting position she wielded it in a wide arc, connecting with Damian's body high up between his legs at the front.

Damian let out a ghostly wail, and collapsed onto his knees in agony, gripping the front of his pants.

Moore scrambled to her feet and retrieved her handcuffs from her belt, and with Damian still incapacitated, she had no trouble cuffing his wrists behind his back.

"One false move from you, matey, and you get this across your skull," she said brandishing the iron bar in his face.

She took her phone out of her pocket and was dismayed to see 'No signal' displayed in small white letters at the top.

"Right, sunshine, we're going for a walk. You first, and if you put a foot wrong or try anything, I'll whack you so hard across the head you won't wake up till next month. Got it?"

Damian, still partly doubled over from his earlier injury, mumbled something, and the unlikely pair set off up along the road to the top of the hill where Moore hoped there would be a decent mobile signal.

Progress was slow. Damian was more or less stumbling along, and Moore was very wary of him, half expecting him to turn on her at any moment. In truth, she thought, if he did decide to have a go, he could probably overpower her quite easily, despite the handcuffs and the fact that she had a weapon.

Eventually, they reached the top of the hill, and Moore instructed her captive to sit on one of the small concrete bollards that demarked the site of the petrol station from the road. She stood close, but not so close as to allow Damian the opportunity to lunge at her. Taking her phone back out from her pocket, she was pleased to see that there was indeed a relatively strong signal now that they were clear of the side of the hill, but the phone's battery was almost totally depleted.

Concerned that the thing might run out of power before she could summon help, she dialled Burke's number. It was answered on the third ring by his familiar voice.

"Hi Fiona, what's up?"

"Don't say anything – just listen. I'm at the petrol station at the top of the Long Hill near Kilmacanogue. I have a suspect with me in handcuffs. I need backup immediately, and my car is buggered."

"Jesus! How the hell did you get into that mess?"

"Aidan, my phone is almost out of juice. Don't ask. Just get me some help. NOW!" And with that, her phone went dead.

Damian had heard the conversation in full, and realised that at some stage in the very near future he would be taken into custody. He also realised that thanks to the stupid woman at Braemore House, he had probably left enough evidence behind him to convict him of all three murders. If he wanted to avoid all that, he would have to act now, and act decisively.

Damian bent forward in his sitting position on the bollard and started to moan loudly.

"I think you've ripped me kidneys. I'm in agony here," he cried, putting as much pathos into his voice as he could.

"I need help. I could die. At least let me lie down," he said.

Moore didn't know how hard she had struck him earlier, but she knew it had been quite forceful. She might indeed have done some serious damage, and although she was glad to have the man under control now, it wouldn't look good if he croaked in these circumstances. Anyway, he looked pathetic, and of little danger as he sat there moaning with his hands secured behind his back.

"I need a drink of water," Damian implored, sounding weak and disorientated.

Moore approached him gingerly. She couldn't give him a drink – not yet anyway – not until reinforcements arrived, but she might be able to make him a bit more comfortable. She kept the bar at the ready in case he was fooling, but she was fairly sure that he was in pretty poor condition. As she approached where he was sitting curled up on the little concrete stump, Damian sprang up in front of her, his head smashing into her chin and knocking her backwards to the ground where she landed, out cold.

His immediate instinct was to get away, but before he made a run for it, he needed to sort out a couple of things. Firstly, he took Moore's mobile phone out of her pocket and smashed it underfoot, kicking the broken remains as far as he could across the road. Then he got the iron bar out from where her fingers were curled around the shaft. He couldn't strike her with it due to his hands being tethered behind his back, but as she was obviously unconscious in any case, he left her alone. He set off limping back down the hill. If he could just get to his car before the police arrived, and get the handcuffs off, he just might be able to get away.

Chapter Twenty-Seven

Burke lost no time in mustering resources to go to the aid of his colleague. He used the Garda emergency code to stimulate immediate action, and within seconds of his call, Gardaí from Bray and Greystones were scrambling for their vehicles to rush to Moore's assistance. One of the vehicles from the checkpoint on the N11 also got permission to respond, and they set off up the Long Hill at warp speed.

Damian was running, half-stumbling towards his car when he heard the first Garda vehicle approach. He threw himself into the ditch, and crouched down low, and the speeding squad car shot past him – the occupants clearly focused on the road – without seeing him. He had to repeat the manoeuvre again when the second car approached, but then he was at the entrance to the quarry, and he hobbled around behind the mound of gravel, hiding himself from the road.

Then, using the crowbar he still had in his hands wedged between two enormous boulders, he positioned himself in such a way that he could snap the chain joining the two sides of the handcuffs. Using all his strength, he levered the bar between the cuffs, and with a satisfying snap, the two sides parted.

Damian resisted the temptation to set off immediately. He needed to think, and he needed to get his breathing and heartbeat back to somewhere near normal, otherwise he could easily crash the car which was the last thing he wanted. As he sat in the old Nissan nursing his bruised wrist, with his metabolism slowly returning to normal, he forged a plan in his head.

* * *

When the Gardaí got to the petrol station at the top of the hill, Moore was slowly coming around. She was very woozy, but as her head began to clear, she did a mental check of her limbs, hands and feet, and concluded that there was no major damage. But she had a thundering headache, and she was very, very cold.

One of the young Gardaí got a blanket from the car and put it around her shoulders. Then, with her permission, he gingerly helped her to sit into the squad car where the heater, now turned up fully, soon began to thaw her out.

"We'd better get you an ambulance, Sergeant," the young man said, getting on the radio to control who would in turn despatch an ambulance from Loughlinstown Hospital which was not very far away.

"I'm OK really. Did you catch yer man?"

"No, Sarge. We didn't see anyone at all. And we just wanted to get to you as quickly as possible."

"Damn. He can't be very far away, and he's handcuffed, so he won't get far. Can you send one of the cars back down the hill to look out for him?"

"Yes, OK. You stay here with me, and I'll send the others back down."

* * *

Damian's natural instinct was to try and get home, but he realised that that would be a foolish move. There would be more roadblocks, and they may even have figured out where he lived by now, so he'd have to revert to plan B. The Wicklow hills had accommodated many fugitives over the years going right back to when the rebels held out against the British in the nineteenth century, so he reckoned it would do the same for him for a short while at least.

He started his car, and eased it back onto the road, and set off up the hill. He knew it was a risk, but he figured that the cops would be pre-occupied with their injured Sergeant, and he would just drive by slowly, hoping not to attract their attention.

But he had miscalculated. The second squad car, coming down the hill, spotted the old Nissan and recognised the partial number plate.

"Christ! That's him! Quick, turn around – get after him!" the Garda in the passenger's seat said.

The driver executed a rapid three-point turn, and putting on his blue lights, gave chase. The second Garda in the car tried to radio ahead to the other car at the petrol station to intercept Damian, but again, there was no reception.

When Damian saw the Garda car coming up behind him with its lights flashing, he panicked. He floored the accelerator, and with a lot of smoke, and much complaint from the old, tired engine, his car took off in more or less a straight line with the Guards in pursuit. Once on top of the bog, Damian was able to increase his speed, and as the road was narrow, there was no opportunity for the following Garda car to get alongside or in front of him. He drove on, with the speedometer now showing 80 mph, and the car bouncing wildly on the uneven road surface.

All was going well till they reached the S bends on the road close to the foot of Djouce Mountain. Damian wasn't very familiar with the road at this point, and the bends took him by surprise. As he steered the car to the right, he stamped on the brakes to try and slow down, and the car lost its tenuous grip on the road, hitting the ditch on the left, and rolling twice in the air before coming to rest on its roof in a shower of sparks, steam and smoke.

The Gardaí, who were more familiar with the road, had slowed down in anticipation, and simply witnessed the demise of Damian's Nissan as spectators, bringing their own vehicle to a halt at a safe distance from the melee. When Damian's car had come to rest, they hopped out and approached the upturned wreck. Damian had blood all over his face, but the car's airbags had saved him from total annihilation, and he lay there, crumpled and bleeding, moaning softly, as the two Gardaí extricated him from the twisted metal, lest it should burst into flames and burn the man to death.

* * *

DI Aidan Burke arrived just as they were helping Sergeant Fiona Moore into the ambulance. She was fully *compos mentis* by this stage, and some colour had returned to her face thanks to the ministrations of the young Garda who had come to her rescue.

Burke sat into the ambulance with his colleague.

"Crikey, Fiona, you don't do things by halves, do you? Are you OK?"

"I'll live. Stupid of me to let the little scum bag get away. I don't suppose you've heard if they've caught him yet?"

"No, I don't think so. But he can't have got far. And he probably still has your bracelets on, so he won't be hard to spot. But listen, how are you feeling? Really," Burke said.

"I'm OK. I feel a bit dizzy, and my eyesight's a bit squiffy – like I've had too many vodkas – I wish! But it's probably only mild concussion. I'll be fine."

"Well, you best get off and have a check-up. I'll stay here and tidy up. Have you got your phone?"

Moore searched her pockets.

"No, it's gone. He must have taken it."

"There's what looks like a few bits of a phone out here on the ground. Maybe he just stamped on it and threw it away. I'll see if any of the young lads has a spare. Hang on there a minute."

Burke was back a few moments later and handed Moore an old iPhone.

"Here, use this for now. I've called my phone on it, so my number is in there. I want to stay in touch. OK – off you go."

In an uncharacteristic gesture, Burke leaned in and planted a soft, quick kiss on Moore's forehead, before turning away and closing the rear doors of the ambulance.

As he re-joined the rest of the crew, word of the accident came in over the radio. Another ambulance was summoned, and Burke told the Gardaí who had been in pursuit of Damian when he crashed to remain there – he would be along shortly.

* * *

Burke arrived at the crash scene a few minutes later. The Gardaí had helped Damian into the back seat of their vehicle, and had administered basic first aid. The suspect was drifting in and out of consciousness, but Burke felt that could be an act to spare him from awkward questioning.

Burke spoke to the Garda who had been driving, and heard the story of the pursuit, and how it had come to an end.

"You'll have to fill in a detailed report. Superintendent Heffernan isn't keen on us running people off the road, no matter what the circumstances. Have you got dashcam footage?"

"Yes, sir," the young man replied.

"Well, make sure it's preserved. Well done anyway – he's a nasty piece of work."

Chapter Twenty-Eight

Burke, Moore and Lawler got together at ten the following morning. Moore had been examined at Loughlinstown Hospital and discharged at around three o'clock in the morning. She had to get a taxi home, as her car was still halfway up the mountain stuck in the fence. She'd get a recovery truck out to it later.

"So, what have we got then?" Burke said.

Lawler looked at Moore, signalling that he expected her to outline the details of their case against Damian.

"Well at least we now know who he is. Damian Coleman, and as predicted he lives in a flat on South Lotts Road. The lads from Irishtown are going around there this morning with a forensic team to give the place a good going over. Apart from that, we don't know much else about him."

"Is he definitely the man who bumped off the three old dears?" Lawler said.

"Looks like it. But we'll have to build a strong case. If he refuses to talk, it's not going to be easy. It'll be all down to forensics as usual. Who wants to interview him this morning?" Burke said.

"I'm happy to do that with Dónal," Moore said. "I'm just dying to renew our acquaintance. At least we've got him banged to rights for assaulting a police officer – we might even stretch it to attempted murder, or GBH at the very minimum."

"But they won't even remand him on that one, unless we can demonstrate that he's a danger to the public or a flight risk. Do you think we could get the woman from Braemore House to do an identity parade with him?" Burke said.

"Maybe. But would her testimony be any good? A decent defence barrister would shred it in no time – you know, old woman, poor eyesight, darkened room etc., etc. It might be better not to put her through that. Let's see what forensics bring back from her room," Moore said.

"I'll have to go and brief Heffernan. There'll be a lot of media interest in this whole thing, and you know how he likes to be kept informed. So, what exactly have we got on Mr Coleman – in hard evidence terms?"

"Not all that much in fairness. We have the shoe prints from Dartry Manor. We may be able to match those to the shoes he was wearing last night, or if not, then they will probably be in his flat. He hasn't left any fingerprints anywhere. But there is the remaining phial of morphine. If we find that at his home, then that could tie him in. And there's the statement from the man who saw him mooching around the empty house in Glenageary. He'll probably be able to identify him," Moore said.

"It all sounds a bit circumstantial to me. Let's see what the boss says. You two go and make Mr Coleman feel as uncomfortable as possible. We'll catch up later."

Moore asked the desk sergeant to bring Damian Coleman to an interview room in Store Street Garda station, and asked if a solicitor had been provided for the man.

"Yes, Fiona. Teddy Cooper is here. He's just having a cup of tea."

"Thanks Danny. We'll be down in a few minutes."

* * *

Teddy Cooper was one of a handful of duty solicitors that were assigned to those who had been arrested in Dublin's city centre. He was a man in his early thirties, and Moore had always found him to be quite agreeable, while still protecting the rights of his clients with a good degree of professionalism. But he was better than some of the breed who objected to every word the Gardaí said, and constantly tried to portray their charges as whiter than white, often despite the interviewees' long history of criminal activity.

Moore and Lawler spent forty minutes questioning Damian Coleman about the incident the previous night with Moore herself, and the deaths of the old ladies in the three care homes, but Coleman remained resolutely silent.

They tried everything they knew to get him to open up. They played good-cop-bad-cop with him, they implied threats, without being specific, and they cajoled, hinting at a lesser punishment if he was willing to co-operate – all to no avail whatsoever. He said not a single word.

Realizing that they were wasting their time, the two Gardaí left the room, but Moore waited a few moments outside for Teddy Cooper to appear.

"Fancy a coffee?" she said. "We can go across the road if you like."

"Yes, OK," Cooper said, and the two made their way outside to the Café Sol on the corner opposite the station. Moore bought Cooper and herself a cappuccino apiece, which were delivered after much hissing and gurgling from the complex machine being skilfully manipulated by the barista.

"What's the story with yer man, Teddy?" Moore said when they were seated uncomfortably on stools that were just a shade too high.

"He's said nothing to me either, I'm afraid. He's quite odd. Usually, they're mad keen to establish their innocence with their solicitor at least, but this guy just sat there. I'm not sure what to make of it. Are you going to charge him?"

"Dead right. We have him banged to rights for the assault on me. When he was eventually captured after all, he still had a pair of my handcuffs dangling from his scrawny wrists, so he can't very well get out of that. But we want him for the murder of the old girls too. But I'll be honest with you, off the record, the actual evidence is pretty thin," Moore said.

"Forensics, Sergeant, forensics. That's what'll do it – if it was him at all. Let the scientists nail him for you. Anyway, I must be off. I have two more delightful young men to represent before lunch!"

* * *

Burke sat uneasily in front of Superintendent Jerome Heffernan's spacious desk. It wasn't that his chair was uncomfortable – far from it – it was just that he sensed that his boss was not in a good mood, and was in some way dissatisfied with his performance.

Heffernan looked up from the papers he had been studying.

"Right, let's be having you, Aidan. What have you got on this fella downstairs? Can we pin him to the murders of the elderly women?"

Burke outlined the events of the last twenty-four hours to his boss, who seemed to be getting more and more agitated as the story unfolded. When Burke had finished, Heffernan looked him straight in the eye.

"In other words, Aidan, you have bugger all for me to take to the DPP, isn't that right?"

"Not exactly. We have him on the assault of Sergeant Moore. And we may be able to get him remanded while we sort out the forensics. The lads are going over his house as we speak, and when we find out where he works, we'll give that the once over too."

"Hmph. I've had the AC on as well. I managed to dodge his call, but I'll have to ring him back soon. What do you think I should tell him?" Heffernan said.

"Tell him we have a suspect in custody, and that we are hoping to have him remanded while we work up the evidence," Burke said.

"Not very reassuring, is it? He's convinced his mother is going to be bumped off at any minute. I don't suppose you'd like to talk to him?"

"Eh, no, sir, that's fine. I'll leave that to your superior diplomatic skills, if it's all the same."

"Thanks a lot. Right, well away with ye then and get enough to nail this bastard good and proper. And no shortcuts or slip-ups, Aidan. If this fella gets away on us, we'll all be heading for the Aran Islands."

"Yes, sir. I'll get on with it then."

Chapter Twenty-Nine

"Boss, can I have a word?" Moore said as DI Burke reappeared from his meeting with Superintendent Heffernan.

They went into Burke's office, and sat down.

"How's himself?" Moore asked.

"Ah, you know. The AC has been bending his ear, so he's all sweetness and light! What's up anyway?"

"Declan Lowry from forensics was on. He wants us to go over there. He doesn't want to leave the lab – there's a lot of stuff coming in since early on," Moore said.

"OK. Grab your jacket. How are you feeling by the way?"

"Ah, I'll be grand. It won't stop me looking for lots of sympathy though."

"Good luck with that!" Burke said, smiling broadly.

* * *

"Hi, folks. Come on in," Lowry said, gesturing them to come over to a bench where a number of items were laid out.

"You've been busy," Moore said surveying the array of stuff.

"Always, Sergeant, always. Let's start with Mrs Dunne's room," he said walking to one end of the bench.

"We recovered some blood smudges from the door jamb, which we presume belong to your client. Unfortunately, there's not enough for a DNA test that would stand up to scrutiny. You need 3ml for the courts, otherwise the defence will tear it apart."

"Any prints?"

"No. He was wearing nitrile gloves, it seems. But don't despair, there is something else."

"Go on," Burke said. He didn't like to be teased, but it was a well-established characteristic of forensic officers.

"This," he said holding up a round piece of dark wood.

"Mrs Dunne says she bashed your friend on the side of the head with this. And there are some traces on it that may give us enough for a DNA match. I'll have to send it off for analysis. Our equipment isn't up to it."

"OK, well that's something I suppose. Are you hopeful?" Moore said.

"Always hopeful, Fiona, but remember we deal in science – no room for emotion in forensics."

"What else have you got?" Burke said, keen to move the revelations on to something they could actually use.

"Three things, Inspector. Firstly, the lads over at his flat have found a small container with one phial of morphine still in it. It was in a box under his bed along with an unopened hypodermic syringe," Lowry said.

"Excellent," Burke said, and turning to Moore, "we should be able to match that up with the ones that were stolen from Dr Willoughby's."

"Second. That laundry tag that you brought in from the little bonfire in the garden. We got onto all of the industrial laundries – there are only three left in Dublin thanks to the popularization of domestic washing machines. They told us that tag is related to a school up beyond Ranelagh. Hang on a sec," he said, reaching for a clipboard where sheets of paper were attached, "yes, here we are, Saint Cyprian's, just off Belgrave Square. It's quite a big place from what I can recall. And there were some payslips from there at his flat too, so I guess he probably works at the school."

"Nice one. And finally?" Moore said.

"Finally, Sergeant, shoes. The pattern that we lifted from the base of the fire escape is close to the pattern on your client's footwear."

"Close? What does that mean?" Burke said.

"There's only about a forty percent certainty that it's the same shoe. There just wasn't enough of an impression left in the soil. And it's a very popular brand, so I wouldn't hang your hopes on it," Lowry said.

"So, basically, Declan, we have nothing conclusive to warrant charging him with murder," Burke said.

"That's up to you, Inspector. I just gather whatever evidence I can find, and connect the dots as best I can. But we're not done yet. We still have his car to work on – or what's left of it – and I'm sure we'll get more from his workplace and his flat."

"Hmm... OK, well, keep us posted. We better get back and see about processing the assault charge – see if we can get him remanded."

* * *

Back at Store Street they charged Damian with assaulting a police officer, dangerous driving, impeding the Gardaí in the course of their duty, and a few other minor charges. He was due to appear at the district court at three o'clock, and Moore decided she would accompany him to see if they could get their chief suspect remanded.

Damian was escorted to a waiting Ford Transit minibus and driven the short distance up along the quays to the court where Judge Jacintha Allen was presiding. Damian spoke simply to confirm his name and address, and Moore read out the charges.

Teddy Cooper stood up when the charges had been read out and applied for bail.

Moore responded quickly, and decisively.

"Judge, the Gardaí are opposing bail on this occasion. We believe that the suspect is a danger to the public, and he works in a school where he has access to young children. He may also be a flight risk."

"Sergeant, you know the rules. Unless you can produce some compelling evidence that your suspect represents a clear and present danger to society, or that he is likely to interfere with witnesses, then I have no alternative but to bail him."

"Yes, but we will be bringing much more serious charges over the next few days, your honour," Moore said.

"That's as maybe. But I have to act on the charges you have brought here today – not some possible future scenario, and from what you have told me, I am inclined to grant bail on the basis that Mr Coleman surrenders his passport, and reports to Irishtown Garda Station three times a week until his trial. When, and if, you prefer additional charges, then no doubt we'll all be here again and I will review the position. Bail is granted on the prisoner's own surety." With that, Jacintha Allen banged her gavel on the bench and the hearing was over.

Moore looked across to Teddy Cooper, who just shrugged his shoulders as if to say 'sorry'.

* * *

"How did that go?" Burke said as Moore came back in from the court.

"It didn't. That silly woman Jacintha Allen only let him out on bail. What's been going on here?"

"Shit! That's all we need. Look, can you take Dónal and get out to the school where chummy works? Bring someone from forensics with you and let them have a go over his workplace. I'd better go back upstairs and brief Heffernan. I don't imagine he'll be too pleased."

"Right. I'll call in if we find anything of interest."

* * *

The school was emptying out when Moore drove into the grounds. Classes had obviously finished for the day, but some enthusiastic pupils were lining up on the single playing field for a game of some sort, all togged out in striped sports gear.

Lawler went off to hook up with the forensic officer who had travelled separately to the school, and arrived first. Moore headed for the office by following the signs, and when she went in Mrs Ketterick was at her usual spot, manning the desk.

Moore introduced herself and asked to see whoever was in charge, although she judged from the demeanour of the woman that she undoubtedly ran the place without getting any of the credit.

"That would be Mr Counihan. He's the headmaster, Sergeant. If you'd like to wait here, I'll tell him you'd like to see him, though he is rather busy today," Ketterick said, giving Moore a rather disdainful look.

The woman disappeared in through a polished brown mahogany door, and emerged a few seconds later followed by the headmaster.

"Please, come in, Sergeant. How can we help you?" the man said, gesturing Moore into his office, or 'study' as he preferred to call it.

Moore sat down opposite Counihan at his nice old antique desk. The room reminded her of the headmaster's room at her own school where she had been chastised more than once for breaking some of the more menial, and to her, ridiculous, school rules when she was a slightly rebellious teenager.

"Can you confirm that a Mr Damian Coleman works here, Mr Counihan?"

"Damian, yes, of course. He's our groundsman and handyman, but I haven't seen him around today. He's usually here on Mondays."

"That's because we have him in custody, sir. Or to be more accurate, we did have him in custody. He's out on bail as we speak."

"Good Lord! Are you serious? What on earth is he supposed to have done?"

"There are various charges, headmaster. But can I ask you what you know of the man? Has he worked here long?"

"Oh, let me see, yes he has. It must be five years or more now. But what has he done, Sergeant? Given that this is a school, I think we have a right to know, don't you?"

"He's been charged with assaulting a police officer – namely me – and a number of other related charges, but I should tell you that we are pursuing investigation of some much more serious matters. I can't go into details. We expect to bring further charges over the next few days," Moore said.

"I see. Do you think we should suspend him from work?"

"That's up to you, headmaster. I'm sure you have some protocol or guidance from the Department of Education that you can follow. I just wanted to let you know. Oh, and we have a forensic team examining his workshop here at the moment. We found some evidence that we believe came from the school that's connected to one of the other crimes we believe he may have committed."

"This is all most distressing, Sergeant, and if I may say, your keeping me in the dark isn't helping. What am I supposed to do if he turns up here, tomorrow say, expecting to work as usual?"

"If I were you, I'd make some excuse and send him home. We don't believe he's particularly dangerous – not unless you live in an old folks' home in any case – and we're keeping a close eye on his movements. But I have to ask, have you had any issues with Mr Coleman while he was working here?"

"Issues – what sort of issues?"

"You know, petty theft, insubordination, tardiness or unexplained absences – that sort of thing," Moore said.

"Not that I'm aware of, but you'd need to ask Mrs Ketterick for any details. I have enough to be doing without checking up on the groundsman every day."

"Yes, all right. Well thank you for your time, Mr Counihan. I'll let you know if there are any further developments."

Chapter Thirty

"So, what you are telling me, Inspector, is that your prime suspect in four murder cases is now free to walk the streets, and you have only the flimsiest evidence to link him to any of them, is that the way it is?" Heffernan said, taking a loud slurp from his cup of tea.

"Not quite, sir. I'm confident the forensic people will be able to place him at the scene of at least one of the murders later this week. And we're continuing to gather evidence from the place where he works and his flat. Oh, and we still have his car to analyse. They're bringing it in this afternoon."

"And just what exactly am I supposed to tell the AC? His mother may be at risk in that place up in Dartry. If anything happens up there again, we'll all be back on the beat!"

"I know it's tricky, sir, but we're working flat out on it. And I have a tail on him now, so he won't be getting up to anything for the moment," Burke said.

"He'd better not be! Look, Aidan, I'm not joking here – we need to bring this to an end soon. Today, preferably, but if not, then tomorrow or Wednesday. Don't let me down on this one, Aidan. There're no prizes for second place. Got it?"

"Yes, of course, sir, I understand. I'll sort it, don't worry."

* * *

Damian was furious. He didn't know whether to be angrier with himself, or that bitch cop that had caught up with him last night.

"How the hell did she know where to find me? That was damn bad luck. And now I have no car either, thanks to her," he said to himself as he sat in a café near the courthouse. His mind was racing. Could he go back home? Was it safe, and what about work? He didn't know what to do, but after he'd downed another strong black coffee, some ideas began to form in his mind.

He'd walk back to Ringsend and do a recce on his flat. If it all looked nice and peaceful with no cops about, he'd go in and pack a knapsack with some essentials and then take off for a few days. He didn't have to report to the Garda station until at least Wednesday, so he should be OK. That would give him time to form a plan.

An hour and a half later he'd done exactly what he had said he would. The Gardaí had obviously been over his place with a fine-tooth comb, and they weren't too fussy about leaving it in an even worse mess than it was in before. The fifth phial of morphine was gone of course, but at least they hadn't found the stash of cash that he had hidden behind a brick in what used to be the outside toilet in the back yard of the small cottage.

He didn't like the fact that he was on foot. He knew that there was a car scrapyard not too far away up near Clanbrassil Street, and if he was lucky he might be able to buy an old banger that was still just about going for a couple of hundred quid.

The young Garda who had been assigned the task of following Damian kept a safe distance as they both walked up along the canal. He was dressed in plain clothes, but had his radio in his jacket pocket. When they had just got beyond the junction of Mespil Road and Burlington Road, the young officer's radio burst into life. When control had established where he was, and what he was doing, he was instructed to break off and go immediately to Baggot Street where two thugs had held up a chemist shop using a hammer. Without any hesitation he did what he was told. With a bit of luck, he might even manage to catch one or both of them.

Damian continued up along the canal unaware of the drama that had unfolded behind him. He turned right at Harold's Cross bridge, and walked on down to Clanbrassil Street and the old scrapyard. He arrived just as the place was shutting up shop for the night.

Inside, a man in his late fifties, dressed shabbily, and with several days' growth of beard on his grease-stained face was wiping his hands on a dirty rag.

"Hi there. I was just wondering if you have anything cheap that's still going?" Damian said to the grumpy old man.

"What sort of money are we talking?" the old guy said.

"Depends what you've got," Damian said, casting his eyes around to examine the stock. Over by the huge rusty old crane that was used to lift the scrap cars into the crusher, he spotted a maroon Ford Fiesta that was waiting its turn to be reduced to a cube of twisted, rusty, steel.

The man saw where Damian's eyes were focused.

"Aye, that one's still going. There's no tax or anything mind, and the brakes are a bit soft, but she'd do you if you're careful with her."

"How much do you want for it?" Damian said, trying to appear indifferent.

"Ah, she's yours for two-fifty. We don't get much call for parts for them yokes anymore."

"I'll give you a hundred, as long as you have the key," Damian said.

"Feck off! The wheels are worth more than that!"

"As you wish, but it's a fair offer," Damian said and stared at the man. The old guy didn't stir, and when what seemed like an age had passed, Damian turned and started walking towards the corrugated iron gate that led back out onto the street.

"OK then, you tight arse. Give me a hundred and twenty and take her away," the man said.

Damian smiled, and reached into his trouser pocket. He turned away from the man so that he wouldn't catch a glimpse of how much Damian had in cash, and peeled off six twenty-euro notes. Turning back, he held them up for the man to see, but instead of handing the money to him, he walked over to the Fiesta, pulled open the driver's door which creaked loudly and sat in. The car was tidy enough inside. There was a tear in the upholstery of the front passenger's seat with bright yellow foam peeking out from the grey velour, but apart from that, and a smell of old cigarettes, it looked to be in reasonable condition. The key was in the ignition switch, so Damian twisted it, and the little car groaned into life with a bit of wheezing and a cloud of blue smoke.

The old guy was now standing holding the driver's door, for fear that his customer would drive off without paying him, but Damian didn't need that kind of trouble, so he handed over the money which disappeared quickly into the man's overalls.

"We don't do test drives," the old guy said with a toothy grin. "Now be off with ye," he said, waving Damian off the premises.

The little car was better than Damian had expected. The brakes were fine if you pumped the pedal a few times, and the lights, indicators and windscreen wipers worked, although there was no water in the washer bottle. Damian drove to a big self-service garage with a large shop attached that was a bit further up the canal going towards the Naas Road. He drove around the back of the building where, as he suspected, a cold-water tap was stuck on the outside wall. Filling an empty Coke bottle that he found on the floor of the car, he popped open the bonnet and filled the windscreen washer bottle to the brim. He then undid the radiator cap, and topped up the grimy water in that too. He dipped the oil, and although it was very black, there was plenty of it. Next, he drove around to the front of the place and put twenty litres of fuel in the tank before pumping the tyres up to their optimal pressure using the air hose provided by the garage.

When he went inside to pay for the fuel, he bought some basic foodstuffs too, so by the time he had finished, he was well set up for what lay ahead. If he hurried up a bit, he might just be in time for what he had in mind.

* * *

"God give me strength!" Moore said, slamming down the phone at her desk.

Dónal Lawler, who was just packing up to go home, said, "What's up, Sarge?"

"They've only fucking lost Damian Coleman, haven't they? The numpty that was tailing him got called away to an armed robbery. I ask you – whose bright idea was that, I wonder?"

"Shit! Is there a watch on his place?"

"No, just a periodic drive by. They don't have the resources for a 24-7 obbo. Anyway, at least he's still on foot, so he won't get far. I've had enough of this for today. I'm going home."

"OK. See you in the morning then."

Chapter Thirty-One

Damian got back into the city soon after six o'clock, and parked his newly acquired vehicle where he could see the exit from Store Street Garda station without appearing obvious. He was getting used to the foibles of the little Ford, and wondered why a vehicle which was really in quite good condition should be going to the crusher.

He'd only been sitting there for a few minutes when he saw Detective Sergeant Moore exit the car park and turn into the slow evening traffic. Damian started the car and eased into the stream himself, three cars behind her.

The city traffic was moving slowly, as it was just nearing the end of rush hour, and Damian had no difficulty keeping up with Moore. They drove up along O'Connell Street, around by Parnell Square onto Dorsett Street, and then moved a bit more quickly on towards Glasnevin. At the Whitworth Road junction Moore turned left and almost immediately right into a maze of narrow streets flanked on both sides by single-storey red-bricked cottages. Damian became concerned that she would spot that she was being followed, so he eased back a little, keeping her own Ford Focus just barely in sight. Moore stopped outside a two-storey red-bricked house on one of the side streets, and parked her car. Damian parked on the other side of the same street, and watched, getting down low in the driver's seat, hoping she wouldn't see him. But Moore was pre-occupied with getting inside, and she didn't notice her stalker who was taking careful note of the number of her house.

A few minutes after she had disappeared inside, when he was sure she wasn't going to re-emerge, he got out and went across to the property. There were three bells positioned vertically beside the front door, and 'Moore' was written in blue marker on the topmost one.

Damian then put phase two of his plan into action. He found a phone box easily enough at the end of the road, and used it to call Store Street Garda station.

"Hello, hello. You know that guy you were looking for – the one that you had the e-fit in the paper for?"

"Yes, sir. May I ask who's calling please?" Sergeant Danny Wallace said.

"Well I've just seen a guy that looks an awful lot like him up near the old folks' home on the airport road. You know, the one beside the Skylon Hotel."

"Right, sir. How long ago was that?"

"Just now, mate."

With that Damian hung up and made his way hastily back to his car. He fetched the piece of rope that he had brought with him from his own flat from the rucksack in the boot. He then crossed the road, and hunkered down at the side of Moore's car away from her front door and waited.

As he had predicted, less than two minutes later, Moore came crashing out of the house, struggling to put on her jacket. As she approached her own car, Damian ducked around from where he had been hiding and got behind her. He passed the rope over her head, and tightened it around her neck, saying, "Now, you bitch. See how you like it!"

Moore wasn't sure exactly what was happening or who was on the other end of the ligature that was slowly choking her, but her natural instincts and comprehensive training kicked in pretty quickly. Most people would try to move forward to get away from their assailant while scrabbling at their neck to try to relieve the pressure – but Moore did the opposite. She used all the purchase her shoes could provide on the footpath, and pushed back hard against Damian, causing him to lose his balance and topple backwards onto the path.

Moore came down with him, but taken by surprise by the unexpected turn of events, and in an effort to break his fall onto the hard surface, Damian let go of one end of the rope as he fell. Moore then twisted around just enough to bring Damian's face into view, and using a technique that often disgusted her during her training, she stabbed her right thumb and forefinger deep into Damian Coleman's eyes. Instinctively, Damian's hands went to his face as he yelped in pain. He tried to open his eyes, but it was impossible. Now blinded, at least temporarily, he became disoriented, and flailed about in agony, as Moore, regaining her composure, handcuffed the man where he lay.

"You've blinded me, you bitch!"

"I certainly hope so, Damian. But I'm afraid it won't last very long. It'll be very sore for a few hours, but you'll be fine, don't worry."

It didn't take long for reinforcements to arrive once Fiona Moore got on the radio to her colleagues. Damian, who was slowly recovering from his temporary blindness, although both eyes were very bloodshot, was blaspheming and shouting as they put him away in the Garda van. Moore collected the rope he had used to attempt to strangle her and put it in a plastic evidence bag. She was a bit shook up, but she was delighted to have captured the man that they had been pursuing, and to put an end to his murderous antics.

* * *

When they got back to Store Street, Damian Coleman was booked in again by the desk sergeant, and placed in a cell. Moore went upstairs where Dónal Lawler was still at his desk.

"Hey! Well done you! That's fantastic, Sarge. Does the boss know?" Lawler said.

"Not yet. Give me a minute to catch my breath. Anything new here?"

"Forensics have been back on. They are pretty certain they'll be able to use the evidence from that piece of wood that the old woman had to defend herself against him. They'll have a definite answer tomorrow."

"Great. Get back on to them, will you. We need a team out at my place. Coleman had a car – that's the only way he could have found out where I lived. He must have followed me when I went home earlier. Get his keys from the front desk and see if they can find it. And while you're at it, give them this. There's bound to be skin particles on it," she said, handing him the bag with the piece of cord in it.

"I'm going to call Aidan and let him know."

Burke was delighted when he heard the news and offered to come back into the station to help them celebrate, but Moore put him off the idea. She just wanted to make sure all the evidence was properly captured, then she was going home for a long soak in a hot bath to get any traces of that slimy bastard off herself.

"Would you like me to come round to yours?" Burke said.

"And what? Scrub my back? No, it's OK thanks, I'm fine."

* * *

The following morning, Burke decided he would interview the suspect. He didn't like the fact that his colleague had been assaulted, and he was keen to face down the perpetrator. Teddy Cooper had also arrived in to ensure that the Gardaí adhered strictly to procedures.

Burke and Lawler both had takeaway coffees when they entered the interview room, and Lawler asked, "Would you like coffee, Damian? Mr Cooper?"

Damian shook his head, and Teddy Cooper declined politely.

"Well now, Damian. I'd like to know why you attacked my colleague outside her home last evening, obviously with the intention of strangling her?" Burke said.

"Really, Inspector, you have no reason to suggest that my client had any intention of killing your colleague, have you?" Cooper said.

"If someone comes up behind you and places a ligature around your neck and then pulls it tight, there can't be much doubt about their intentions, can there?"

Cooper said nothing.

"So, Damian, I'll ask again, why were you trying to kill Sergeant Moore?"

"No comment."

"I see. That's the way it's going to be, is it? And what's all this with you and old ladies – why have you got it in for them?"

"No comment."

This went on for another fifteen frustrating minutes, at which time Burke brought proceedings to a halt. As he was terminating the interview, Teddy Cooper said, "A word outside, Inspector?"

When they got outside the interview room, Lawler went back upstairs leaving Burke on his own with the solicitor.

"What's on your mind, Mr Cooper?"

"I'm just wondering what exactly you've got on him? If you have any real evidence – I mean proper conviction quality stuff – I might be able to get him to open up a bit if we could make an arrangement?"

"Look, Mr Cooper, your client has almost certainly killed three old ladies in cold blood. He's also tried to kill a fourth, and he's had two goes at members of the Guards as well. Just what sort of arrangement had you in mind?"

"Well, at the very least, we'll need to have him psychologically assessed."

"What, the old diminished responsibility trick, you mean?"

"Well, you have to admit, it's a bit weird if he did actually bump off three old dears, don't you think?" Cooper said.

"Right now, Mr Cooper, I'm just keen to get our 'conviction quality' evidence assembled as you call it. I imagine we'll be charging him with three counts of murder before the day is out, and I'd be very much obliged if you would not apply for bail on this occasion."

"Hmph. We'll see," Cooper replied, and walked off.

Chapter Thirty-Two

"How did that go?" Moore said to Burke when he returned from the interview.

"A lot of 'no comment' and bullshit. But the solicitor knows we have him banged to rights. Taylor is looking for a psychological assessment."

"Hmm. OK. Let's get the jump on them on that score. Can we get Dr Coogan in for another interview with him? See if she can't rattle him a bit. And it would stop Cooper getting one of his favourite shrinks to attend," Moore said.

"OK – sounds like a plan. Can you give her a call?"

"Great. Catch you later."

Moore made the call.

Mairéad Coogan was surprised to hear from the officer. Moore explained the position to her, and told her that she had been correct about the profile of their suspect that she had given the Gardaí earlier on, and asked her if she could come in to attend an interview with him.

"I'll have to switch around a few appointments, but I could be with you at, say, three o'clock if that would be any good?" Coogan said.

"Yes, that would be perfect. See you later."

When Moore had set up the interview, she got back on to forensics and spoke to Phil.

"Hi, Phil. I need to know if you've got anything back on the stick from Braemore House."

"Hold on a sec. Yes, here we are. Yep! There's a good match between the traces found on the end of the stick with your suspect – what's his name – Coleman."

"Enough to place him at the scene with no wriggle room?" Moore said.

"Oh, yes. No doubt. Plus, we have the cloth fragment that ties him back to the school where he works."

"OK. But I need something to connect him to the other deaths too. Give me some good news, Phil."

"It's all a bit circumstantial, I'm afraid. We have the original phial that we got under the bed at the scene of the first killing, but there's no DNA or prints. We can match it to the single unused dose we found in the guy's flat though. Would that be enough?"

"No, I don't think so. We need something that ties him either to the victims or the scenes of the crimes. Look, can you go back over everything for me. I'm really stuck on this one."

"Yes, sure, Fiona. I'll get back to you later."

"Thanks, Phil."

* * *

"Do you want to sit in when Dr Coogan gets here?"

"No, not this time. This is really your gig. Unless you think I should?" Burke said.

"No, no. I just don't want you to feel excluded. I'm happy to do it."

While Moore was waiting for Coogan to arrive, she got hold of Dónal Lawler and they went back over each of the killings one by one.

"What is it we're missing, Dónal? The fecker can't be that clever."

"Well, he isn't, is he? After all, you've caught him twice?"

"Don't remind me! But, no, there has to be something more here. What about the CCTV stuff we got from the place in Dartry? Let's have another look at that."

Lawler rummaged in his desk and brought out the DVD that they had recovered from Dartry Manor. He put it into a PC and started it up.

"There was something about an unidentified nurse in this one, if I remember rightly, isn't that right?" Moore said.

"Oh, yes, I remember now. Hang on. Yes – here she is."

"OK. So, if that is Damian Coleman – where is the wig and the outfit? We didn't find it at his flat, or at his workplace."

"Maybe he destroyed them. That's what I would do if I were him," Lawler said.

"Maybe. But why? If he was planning more attacks – which he was – then they could have come in handy, and it wouldn't be too easy to get hold of replacements."

"Hmm... I see what you mean."

"Hang on. What about his car?" Moore said.

"Oh, right. Have forensics not been over it yet?"

"I don't know. I don't think so. I'll get back on to Phil and ask him."

Moore called Phil back immediately.

"Phil, it's me again. Sorry to bother you, but have you been over Coleman's car yet – you know, the old Nissan that was brought in from Calary Bog?"

"No, not yet. We've been concentrating on the other stuff. But I think the car is here OK. Why, what do you think is in it?" Phil said.

"It's just possible that there may be a wig and a nurse's uniform stashed away somewhere. Any chance you could have a look for us? If we could find those, it would tie him into the scene at Dartry Manor."

"OK. I'll put Declan on it and let you know."
"Thanks."

* * *

Dr Mairéad Coogan arrived at the Garda station at five to three and asked for Detective Sergeant Moore. Moore went down to greet her and escort her into the open plan office where the detectives worked.

"Thanks for coming in, Doctor. The man we have in custody is Damian Coleman. We caught him attacking an old woman in a nursing home in Shankill – well, sort of caught him. But it was him OK. And we think that would have been his fourth victim – the other three were murdered, and we're fairly sure it's the same killer."

"I see. And what are you hoping that I might be able to do for you, Sergeant Moore?"

"Oh, do call me Fiona. There's no need to stand on ceremony."

"Thanks, and I'm Mairéad, by the way."

"I'm hoping you might be able to get into his head and open him up a bit. He's all 'no comment' and surly stares at the moment. But there must be a reason why he's going around bumping off old ladies. That's not the kind of thing you come across often – not in my experience anyway," Moore said.

"Hmm... I know what you mean. OK. I'm willing to have a go, but no promises mind you. He could just be totally nuts."

"Ah, that's what we are hoping to avoid. You see I think his solicitor is going to go for an insanity plea, or at least diminished responsibility. I'd like us to be able to knock that one on the head, if you'll excuse the expression."

"Right. Well let's go and talk to him and see what we can get. How does all this work? I haven't done this kind of thing before," Coogan said.

Moore explained that the interview would be recorded, and that Damian would have his solicitor present. She explained that she would keep manners on the solicitor if he tried to shut her down, but not to be put off by it.

Chapter Thirty-Three

The four of them were seated around the table in the interview room. Moore started the tape recorder, and made the usual pronouncements about the time and date, and who was present in the room.

It didn't take long for Teddy Cooper to try and spoil the party.

"Sergeant Moore, I must protest at the way you are conducting this interview. I mean, what qualifications does Dr Coogan have and is she here officially, and if so on whose authority?"

"The Gardaí are quite entitled to have whomsoever they feel can assist them to conduct interviews, as you well know, Mr Cooper, and Dr Coogan wouldn't be here if I wasn't perfectly happy with her qualifications, so can we just get on please."

Cooper gave a short grunt, but said no more for the time being.

"Mr Coleman, I wonder if you could tell us a little about your background – you know, your family? Are your parents still alive?" Coogan asked.

"No comment," Damian replied.

"And may I ask if you have any brothers and sisters?"

"No comment."

This line of questioning went on for some time, with Cooper making the occasional intervention to protest, but he was quickly cut off by Fiona Moore. Dr Coogan was ever so slowly bringing Damian Coleman back in time, and although she was getting no verbal acknowledgement from her questioning, Damian's body language indicated that her questions were having some effect.

Cooper sensed that his client was about to start responding, so he called a refreshment break, much to the annoyance of Moore. But she could hardly refuse, and they agreed on twenty minutes, during which time tea would be served to Damian and the solicitor.

Outside the interview room, Moore had a chance to chat to the good doctor.

"How do you think it's going?"

"Not too bad. I know he hasn't said anything, but he's processing my questions, and I think he's about to start answering. That's why Cooper called a halt. He sensed it too. When we go back, I'm going to start on a slightly different tack, so bear with me."

They were just about to go back into the interview room when Dónal Lawler came down the stairs.

"Sarge, can I have a word?"

"Yeah, sure, Dónal, what's up?"

"Forensics have been back on. They went over Coleman's car, and just like you said, they found the wig and the nurse's uniform in it. It was hidden beneath the spare wheel in the bottom bit of the boot, in a plastic bag."

"Excellent," Moore said with a big smile, "*and?*"

"They're doing it now, but Phil says there'll be plenty of DNA on the wig, and he thinks they may get prints off the bag too. How are you getting on with him?"

"Slowly, but Dr Coogan here is getting somewhere," Moore said.

"Will you print me off a few stills from the DVD showing chummy mincing along the corridor with his back to the camera dressed in his drag outfit, and drop them in to the interview room. And let me know if Phil gets anything more, Dónal."

"Right, Sarge."

When Lawler had departed, Dr Coogan asked Moore if she should change her tactics now that new evidence had come to light.

"No, no I don't think so. Carry on as planned for now. I'll tap your foot under the table if we need a change in direction and then I'll take over. Is that OK?"

"Sure."

* * *

"Tell me, Damian," Coogan said when the interview resumed, "about your first day at school."

Damian looked at the doctor and his eyes flared.

"What, you mean primary school?" he said.

"Yes. What school did you go to when you were four or five years old?"

"The national school, of course. It was just down the road from our house. I went when I was four, didn't I?"

"And tell me what it was like, Damian. Did you enjoy school at that age?"

"It was OK. I had some good mates there, but the teacher was a right old witch."

"What was the teacher's name, Damian?"

"Miss Finnucane."

"In what way was she a witch?" Coogan said.

"She was a twisted dried up old spinster. And she was cruel too."

"Cruel? In what way was she cruel? Did she beat you?"

"Sometimes, yes. And she often used to take the biscuits we brought in for break time and eat them herself. She said they weren't good for us."

"I see. Was she cruel in any other way, Damian?"

Damian looked down at the tabletop, and appeared to be thinking through what he would say next. After a few moments of silence, Dr Coogan prompted him.

"Damian?"

"It's a bit… embarrassing."

"That's OK, Damian, take your time. And don't be afraid of embarrassing us. I'm sure I've heard a lot worse," Coogan said.

"Well, it's like, when we wanted to go to the toilet. She wouldn't let us. She made us hold it in – sometimes the whole morning. And a couple of times, I couldn't, so I wet my pants, and then she'd punish me saying I was disgusting and make me go and stand outside to dry off. All the girls would be laughing at me. It was horrible."

"I see. That was dreadful. Did this happen a lot?"

"A few times."

"And was it just you, or were other pupils given the same treatment?"

"It was mostly me. She seemed to hate me more than the others."

Coogan looked at Moore, who nodded, signalling her to continue.

"Was there anything else that happened at the hands of Miss Finnucane that you can remember, Damian?"

"My radio."

"Your radio? Tell us about that, Damian. What about your radio?"

"I was nine. My mam had saved up and bought me a small transistor radio for my birthday. I'd been on and on about it for ages, and she wanted me to have something nice. It was a small one that just picked up medium wave. But I loved it. It was plastic. Cream-coloured with a little shiny aerial. I used to listen to it at night in bed with an ear thing."

"And what happened with the radio, Damian?" Coogan said.

"I brought it into school one day to show my pals. I was so proud of it. And the witch caught us at break time listening to Radio Caroline. She grabbed it and threw it on the floor and then stamped on it, didn't she?" As Damian told the story, his eyes filled with tears.

Fiona Moore tapped Dr Coogan gently on the foot under the table.

"Is that why you left the radio playing in her room?" Moore asked.

Damian just nodded.

"How did you find Miss Finnucane after all this time, Damian?"

"It was easy really. The school is still there. I contacted them and told them I had been a favourite pupil of hers and that I wanted to look the old girl up to see how she was. They gave me her address straight off, no problem."

"But you didn't go straight to her house, Damian, did you?"

"No, you see. I couldn't. I had to make it look random."

"I think I need a few minutes to confer with my client," Teddy Cooper interjected, "could we say fifteen minutes?"

"Very well, Mr Cooper. Come and find us when you are ready to continue. We'll be upstairs."

* * *

"Inspirational, Doctor. Amazing!" Moore said when they were back upstairs. "Here – let's get a coffee."

"I'm surprised he loosened up so easily, to be honest. But what a terrible old cow his teacher was," Coogan said.

"Yeah, I know. But back in those days, there were very few inspections. Teachers could do more or less what they wanted, and if any of the kids tried to tell their parents, they'd probably get another beating for their trouble."

"What happens now?" Coogan said.

"If I'm not very much mistaken, Cooper will come trotting up offering to make a deal of some kind. But he doesn't know we have the wig. So, I'm not keen to make concessions."

The two women were nursing a mug of hot coffee seated at one of the desks in the open plan when Cooper appeared.

"Coffee, Mr Cooper?"

"Yes, please. Good and strong."

Lawler was sent off to brew another mug for the solicitor.

"So, what's the story?"

"My client is prepared to admit to the killing of Miss Finnucane, but he wants to plead diminished responsibility. He was clearly traumatised from a young age by that wicked woman, and it never left him."

"What about the others?"

"Others? What others?"

"The first two old ladies that were killed in a like manner before Miss Finnucane, and then there's Mrs Dunne who was attacked subsequently, or were they all past teachers of his as well?"

"Have you any evidence connecting my client to those incidents?"

"Yes, we have as it happens. We have a wig that he wore when he was killing Mrs Edel Roberts at Dartry Manor, and we have footprints and other evidence linking him to the others too."

"Why wasn't I told about this?" Cooper said indignantly.

"We only found the wig hidden in the boot of his car while the interview that has just taken place was in progress. Sorry about that," Moore said.

"Well then you won't have had time to connect it to my client, will you?"

"Already done, Mr Cooper. Now why don't you stop pissing about and get down to the nitty gritty."

Dr Coogan tried to make herself invisible.

"What do you mean?" Cooper said.

"We go back into the interview room, and Damian Coleman confesses on record to killing Miss Maeve Finnucane giving us details of how he accomplished that gruesome task. If he confesses to Edel Roberts' killing too, that will do us. He can dress it up anyway he wants, but I need both. Then we'll see about the insanity stuff. OK?"

"Very well. I'll see what I can do. What about the assault on the police officer and the other associated charges?" Cooper said.

"Don't worry about those for now. Let's get the murders sorted out first."

Chapter Thirty-Four

When DI Burke heard that they had secured a confession from Damian Coleman for the two murders – one of which had taken place at Dartry Manor where the AC's mother was in residence, he was well pleased.

He lost no time in updating Superintendent Heffernan, who in turn was delighted to be able to report to his superior that the matter was now resolved.

Coleman was charged with two counts of murder, and this time was remanded in custody while the Gardaí prepared their book of evidence. The DPP decided that there was insufficient material to pursue the case of the other two old ladies, and although Stuart Humphries in particular wasn't happy about it, Moore managed to persuade him that as Coleman would be incarcerated for the rest of his life in any case, and as the Gardaí had scant evidence to connect him to Mrs Humphries' killing, there was little point in making a fuss. When he persisted with his claim that there would be no justice for his mother if the man who had killed her was not tried for it, Moore hinted that if he was intent on making things awkward, certain other matters might come out that would not be to his advantage, so he let it go.

It was over a year later when Damian Coleman stood in the dock at the Central Criminal Court charged with the double murder. He had pleaded not guilty by virtue of diminished responsibility, so the case had to be heard in full, and it was very difficult for the jury listening to the manner in which the man had been essentially tortured by his teacher in his early years.

Coleman's barrister produced a psychologist that made much of the trauma that Damian had endured, and the lasting effect it had on him for the rest of his life, until the pressure boiled over and he acted to avenge the wrongs that had been done to him.

The trial lasted three weeks, and at the end of it the jury took four days to find Damian Coleman guilty of murder.

The judge had been impressed by the psychological evidence that had been presented, and was saddened by Damian's story to the extent that he ordered a full psychological assessment before passing sentence. This took a further four weeks, and when Damian next appeared in court to learn his fate, the judge placed him in Dundrum – the Central Mental Hospital – on an indefinite sentence, but with a codicil that he was not to be eligible for release for at least fifteen years.

While Burke and Moore were pleased with their efforts, the media were not very kind, taking the view that the Gardaí had been slow to act which may have cost two or more of the old ladies to lose their lives.

Superintendent Heffernan took some flak over the coverage, but unofficially, the AC was well pleased with the outcome, and asked that his thanks be passed on down the line.

Cedar Hill never recovered from the scandal. Those who had been in residence slowly departed, either to other facilities or to their graves, and Mrs Phillips found it virtually impossible to attract new customers based on the publicity the home had received. After two years, the place was sold and reconverted into two splendid private houses which sold for an impressive sum.

Dartry Manor and Vico View fared better, and continue to host the elderly and look after them in style to this day.

Andrew McKinley from Braemore House found a way to exploit the recent drama that he and his charges had experienced. He enticed RTE to do a documentary about the whole affair for Primetime, and they paid him handsomely for extensive footage shot at the retirement home, and for his own input.

Burke, Moore and Lawler were soon involved in the never-ending series of crimes that keep them busy in Store Street, and while they didn't forget the strange case of the Care Home Killer, they had much to distract them in the months ahead.

Character List

DI Aidan Burke – a senior detective attached to Store Street station with some personal issues.

DS Fiona Moore – DI Burke's 'bagman' whose main task seems to be to make her boss look good.

Superintendent Jerome Heffernan – a wily old officer who manages upwards and downwards with deftness and subtlety – most of the time.

DC Dónal Lawler – a bright young detective.

Declan Lowry – a forensics officer.

Phil Donnelly – lead forensic officer.

Séan O'Reilly – a civilian worker who does clerical work at Store Street.

Sergeant Marian Byrne – a pretty blonde forensics officer.

Detective Inspector Jim Mulcahy – a member of the Gardaí attached to Irishtown.

Dr Malcolm O'Higgins – the State Pathologist.

Dr Fleming – a GP from Glenageary.

Dr Mairéad Coogan – a Psychologist.

Dr O'Sullivan – part owner of an old folks' home.

Dr Willoughby – a GP from Rathgar.

Mrs Phillips – proprietor of an old folks' home.

Mrs Fidelma Humphries – a resident at an old folks' home.

Stuart Humphries – Mrs Humphries' son.
Dylan Humphries – Mrs Humphries' other son.

Paula and Sally – nurses.

Marcella Kane – an estate agent.

Mrs Edel Roberts – a resident at an old folks' home.

Sister Bernie O'Dea – a nurse.

Miss Maeve Finnucane – a resident at an old folks' home.

Mrs Webster – proprietor of an old folks' home.

Anna – the receptionist at an old folks' home.

Mr Andrew McKinley – proprietor of an old folks' home.

Mrs Dunne – a feisty resident at an old folks' home.

Damian Coleman – groundsman at a large suburban school with a troubled past.

Mrs Ketterick – St Cyprian's school secretary.

Mr Counihan – headmaster at St Cyprian's school.

Sam McIvor – a rotund security guard.

Garda McMullan – a Garda dog handler.

Jack – McMullan's German shepherd dog.

If you enjoyed this book, please let others know by leaving a quick review on Amazon. Also, if you spot anything untoward in the paperback, get in touch. We strive for the best quality and appreciate reader feedback.

editor@thebookfolks.com

www.thebookfolks.com

ALSO IN THIS SERIES

The first murder mystery in this Irish crime fiction series by bestselling author David Pearson.

A man killed in a desolate alley. A woman attacked in her home. And two detectives who must connect these events, and hunt down a killer who doesn't give a damn.

A man is found dead in his car in a forest outside of Dublin. Very dead. There is quite a mess. The police suspect foul play and call in the detectives. It is not long before another body is found in the area. A full-scale murder inquiry is launched. Can DI Aidan Burke and DS Fiona Moore collar the killer?

A man killed in a house fire. Badly burned, but shot before the flames are set. When discovered, the weapon points to a China connection, but are detectives just being led away from a motive far closer to home?

OTHER BOOKS BY DAVID PEARSON

In the Galway Homicides series:

Murder on the Old Bog Road (Book 1)
Murder at the Old Cottage (Book 2)
Murder on the West Coast (Book 3)
Murder at the Pony Show (Book 4)
Murder on Pay Day (Book 5)
Murder in the Air (Book 6)
Murder at the Holiday Home (Book 7)
Murder on the Peninsula (Book 8)
Murder at the Races (Book 9)

Available in paperback and free with Kindle Unlimited

Printed in Great Britain
by Amazon

59049581R00125